THE RICH YOUNG RULER

YOUNG RULER

A BIBLICAL NOVELLA AND OTHER SHORT STORIES

*The journey began here
at 1ˢᵗ P.C.*

Blessings,
Geo Grove

GEORGE GROVE

WESTBOW
PRESS
A DIVISION OF THOMAS NELSON

WestBow Press books may be ordered through booksellers or by contacting:

WestBow Press
A Division of Thomas Nelson
1663 Liberty Drive
Bloomington, IN 47403
www.westbowpress.com
1-(866) 928-1240

ISBN: 978-1-4497-2399-6 (sc)
ISBN: 978-1-4497-2398-9 (e)

Library of Congress Control Number: 2011914360

Printed in the United States of America

WestBow Press rev. date: 9/06/2011

Dedicated to

Rev. Dr. Paul Eckel, *Messenger*

Dr. Kenneth Boa, *Teacher*

ACKNOWLEDGMENTS

This little book would never have come to fruition without the encouragement of Mary Lee, my talented artist wife. Rather than having to put up with my long hours of sweating over the writing - out-of-character for me - she encouraged me to take it up after putting it aside many times. Her 'just do it' attitude with her art work was finally contagious and I got over my acedia. (A monk's word for slothfulness).

My dear friend Suzanne Schwank provided invaluable editorial services of the highest order arising from her extraordinary literary breadth and Biblical depth.

Peter Spanos offered great advice on first person writing and the pace of the book.

INTRODUCTION

The stories that follow are written reflections from sacred reading. These sacred readings are from a tradition that goes back to at least the 3rd or 4th Century. The tradition that came to be called *lectio divina*, (pronounced lexio de-vena), Latin for sacred reading, is still practiced in the church, especially by modern day monks. I was introduced to *lectio divina* during a retreat at the Monastery of the Holy Spirit, a Cistercian/Trappist monastery in Conyers, GA. This ancient way of reading Scripture as a direct means of being spiritually conformed to Christ became a spiritual discipline that transformed my devotional life. At first, the practice of *lectio divina* was gradually integrated into my daily morning devotions. It eventually became a lens through which I view Scripture and through which I approach Scripture with the expectation of encountering God in the very doing of sacred reading. Indeed, at those all too infrequent times that I am truly "in the Spirit", *lectio divina* is the lens through which I see myself and the whole of creation. *Lectio divina* is more than simply reading scripture. It is a way to engage the very word of God that leads from reading to meditation to prayer to contemplation. It is a <u>way</u> more than a step by step process; more accurately, it is <u>the way</u> of the Holy Spirit rather than a mental process under our own mind's control. The ultimate place in *lectio divina* is the place of contemplation, where one is silent before God and awaits His word to us.

Robert Mulholland, in his excellent book "Shaped by the Word", describes this approach to God's word as reading for formation rather than information. *Lectio Divina* has become integral to my own quest for spiritual formation, the way of being conformed to the image of Christ. (Rom 8:29). Perhaps this gift from the past can enrich your devotional life as you journey closer to God, as you become conformed to Christ. Occasionally, I am moved by the Word to an extended time of sacred reading. In these times, I intentionally use my imagination to become more deeply engaged with God's word. One way to do that is to place myself into the narrative, the story that is being told in the scripture passage, the story that is bigger than my own story. Sometimes I put myself in the role of one of the characters in the story and I imagine the experience as if I were really there. The stories that follow come from some of those *lectio divina* experiences where God revealed his word to me in a moving way.

PREFACE

God of Abraham and David, you have planted a profound longing deep within me that no earthly attainment or solace can satisfy. This aspiration is for Your manifest presence, and it draws me to see the world as You meant it to be. The brief Camelot of Solomon's early reign, with its splendor and it's far reaching influence on the nations around Israel, gives me a hint of what you are planning for the future which will not be ephemeral, but will go on into eternity. When I come in contact with the innermost desires of my heart, I must openly admit that this present world is not enough. You have planted one of my feet in this age and the other in the glorious age to come. Keep me in touch with this hunger and thirst for what you plan to bring, so that I will see more clearly that nothing in this world is enough to satisfy this divinely given restlessness.

- Ken Boa

PROLOUGE

The Rich Young Ruler
Luke 18:18-27

18 A ruler questioned Him, saying, "Good Teacher, what shall I do to inherit eternal life?" 19 And Jesus said to him, "Why do you call Me good? No one is good except God alone. 20 "You know the commandments, 'DO NOT COMMIT ADULTERY, DO NOT MURDER, DO NOT STEAL, DO NOT BEAR FALSE WITNESS, HONOR YOUR FATHER AND MOTHER.'" 21 And he said, "All these things I have kept from my youth." 22 When Jesus heard this, He said to him, "One thing you still lack; sell all that you possess and distribute it to the poor, and you shall have treasure in heaven; and come, follow Me." 23 But when he had heard these things, he became very sad, for he was extremely rich. 24 And Jesus looked at him and said, "How hard it is for those who are wealthy to enter the kingdom of God! 25 "For it is easier for a camel to go through the eye of a needle than for a rich man to enter the kingdom of God." 26 They who heard it said, "Then who can be saved?" 27 But He said, "The things that are impossible with people are possible with God."

PART ONE

Nekoda is in a steady trot along the road to Shiloh where I am to meet with the new Rabbi, actually a retired Temple priest. I love this horse. His distinct light brown and white markings on a perfectly proportioned large muscular body invites the envy of my friends. Soon, on this familiar route from Ephraim he will, on his own, move smoothly to a gallop, and when he sees the village, break into a full run - his dark brown mane flowing into my face. I am happy when I ride Nekoda. I am not often so happy.

Arriving at the Synagogue, I am greeted by the new Priest, Asa bar Talmai, in the small courtyard outside the modest two story sanctuary.

"Ah, Ethan bar Phinehas, welcome to Shiloh. It has been a long while since we met."

"Indeed it has" I offer as I dismount and tie Nekoda to a gate post beside a trough of water for the donkeys, and rarely horses, that often bring supplicants to the Synagogue.

"That is a magnificent animal you have there. There are so few horses about – except of course for the Romans."

"Thank you, Nekoda is very dear to me."

Asa sweeps his arm toward the two chairs beside the well, "Come, let's sit out here and enjoy this lovely day."

Asa bar Talmai is a stout man of average height wearing a light priest's robe of linen on this pleasant harvest time day. Asa has a peaceful round face which forms a smile that is almost constant.

1

Deep set eyes are an unusual greenish black and signal an intellect that complements his otherwise beatific countenance. His beard is short and without the double cones favored by the Temple priests. His balding hair and beard are a dark grey, befitting a man of over sixty years. He wears a small four cornered priest's cap.

"Rabbi Asa – is it correct to call a retired Temple priest 'Rabbi'?" He nods yes but I see a slight irritation in his black-green eyes. "Thank you for seeing me today. I know you will soon be visiting Ephraim and please accept my Father's invitation to stay with us a few days when you come."

"But of course." His authentic fixed smile has no sign of the irritation.

"And how is Phinehas bar Ezer? I have grown to know him as a kind and able man over the years."

"My father is well. He has slowed a bit due to age but is still the master of the house ," I say with a hint of humor.

"Well Ethan, as the eldest son of one of the greatest households in Palestine I know you carry the duty of stewarding a wide range of enterprises. From what I have heard of you, Ethan bar Phinehas, your father is blessed to have you as a faithful and able elder son."

"Thank you Rabbi Asa, I could hear no kinder complement."

I continue, "May I ask how you came to Shiloh after retiring as a distinguished Temple priest?" I know this is a prying question that may be uncomfortable for him. The rumor has it that Asa was forced out by the High Priest Caiaphas over some Temple politics.

"May I speak frankly, Ethan?"

"Please do." His signal for confidentiality reminds me that he still serves the High Priest.

Asa continues, "I entered Temple service over 30 years ago, the son and grandson of Levi priests before me. Of course, I was ambitious like many of the other young priests, more intrigued by the power of the priesthood than the holiness of it. Over time it became clear to me that I was distinctly ungifted as a Temple politician. I began to meditate on the holiness of the priesthood and to take more seriously the sanctity of the worship liturgy. God gave me a most valuable and underrated gift: contentment." Asa pauses as if recalling past events.

I sense that he welcomes this opportunity to share his burdens; if that is what they are. It strikes me as unusual that a man twice my age would confide in me as he clearly intends to do. But I am of the ruling class which assumes wisdom at an early age. Or so I've heard.

He continues, now fully engaging me with his penetrating gaze. "When I first entered the Temple service I was befriended by a priest who was as old then as I am now. Zacharias, as I look back on my service, had a great influence on me as a mentor. He had long since accepted his role as a minor priest in the Temple hierarchy; as I did later. His spiritual direction led me to turn away from what I now see as the dark side of the Sadducee priesthood. Like him, I believed the priesthood also offered light to those who entered the Temple to truly worship God."

"What happened to Zacharias," I ask?

"An odd thing. One day, after performing the duties in the Holy Place, he was struck mute. A demon? Who knows. But his Temple service was ended and he retired to up around Nazareth. I never saw him again. There were rumors that he later fathered a child with his wife Elizabeth – a fine woman - but that cannot be true since she was past child bearing years."

"Ethan, let me know if I go on too long." He glances up at the sun to determine the time. It is about the 9th hour.

"I have the afternoon, please go on. In fact I have a religious matter I wish to discuss with you. But first, how did you come to choose Shiloh and Ephraim?"

"I served under High Priest Annas for many years. He is a canny politician and saw the value of having a few priests around with no apparent ambitions. I was one of those. Now his son-in-law Caiaphas is High Priest, even though Annas is still very influential. Oh, pardon me for these Temple matters which I am sure one in your position is already aware of, Ethan."

"Rabbi Asa, we do not pay as much attention to Temple matters as you may think."

With a chuckle Asa says "Good for you!"

"Caiaphas, younger than you, I suppose …

I interrupt: "I am in my 34th year."

"Yes, he is about thirty. He wants some changes, one of which is to put us old priests out to pasture – to get in some young blood, new blood!" Asa says this rather strongly. Herein lies the irritation I saw earlier in the flash of the eyes.

"You were against retiring?" I probed tentatively.

"No, but Caiaphas thought I was and criticized my services – unjustly - suggesting that my mind was elsewhere – or more precisely – nowhere. That was resolved through Annas' regard for me. Caiaphas, under pressure from Annas, gave me my choice of retirement place and the office of Rabbi and Priest Emeritus. I requested Shiloh, even though Jerusalem is my home, because it is a sacred and historic place. This is the very ground of the first Temple in Canaan - where Samuel and Eli served. Of course it is also the place the Philistines captured the Ark of the Covenant. The light side and the dark side. I prefer to see the light."

Asa broadens his smile, " Now, Ethan, what is this religious matter you speak of?"

I inquire, "Do you know of the Torah study group that meets monthly around these parts?"

"Why no. How interesting. I did not know such study groups were still around."

"I know of no others; but this one has met long before anyone remembers. Perhaps Samuel started it," I respond with a slight laugh.

"Oh, so it is a thousand years old!" We both laugh at the improbability.

I continue, "We usually have six or seven men attend – there are ten or twelve altogether from Sadducee families hereabouts. Believe it or not, we actually discuss the Torah and the matters of life under the law. Then dinner and good fellowship afterwards; helped along with our fine Ephraim wine."

Asa responds jovially, "And copious amounts of the Ephraim wine I am sure! The wine from your estate is the favorite in the Temple."

"What an honor. Thank you."

"Asa, last week a Pharisee Rabbi from these parts spoke to us about the afterlife – eternal life he called it. Of course we Sadducees don't believe there is an afterlife, but I found him to be a very winsome speaker and rather persuasive on some points."

Asa interrupts, "They cannot make a case for afterlife from the Torah."

I respond, "He tried, knowing we stand on the Torah alone for our laws. His more interesting comments came from the Psalms and the prophets. I have thought of his claims a lot since the meeting. An afterlife, eternal life, does raise hope within me. You are a learned religious leader, what are your thoughts?"

Asa glances at the sun, "It is getting late. You have raised a matter that will take more time than we have now. I have much to say about this and we can talk when I come to Ephraim – soon. For now, let me say this: I discern that you are one of those men who are on a quest. You have a place in your heart that is not yet filled. Am I wrong?"

"No Rabbi Asa, you are not wrong. But I have no one with whom to explore this, this quest. I am a rich man, I want for nothing. People would think me a fool if I said life did not satisfy me."

"Ethan, you are not alone, in fact, you questors are legion. Let us explore your quest when we next meet. Perhaps I can help you as Zacharias helped me. Meanwhile pray regularly for God to lead you – to lead us. God hears the prayers of a faithful man.

+ + +

I awaken refreshed at the home of my sister Sherah and Baruch, my brother-in-law. He manages our affairs around Shiloh. Baruch has made good profits by increasing trade with merchants far to the east. After breakfast and good-byes, I mount a rested Nekoda for the short ride back home to Ephraim.

With Nekoda at a leisurely pace, I reflect on my meeting with Asa. I admire his wit and his intelligence. He is not a prideful man, as I had probably expected, because most of the Temple priests I have known appear absorbed with self importance. I hope he will become a mentor, someone I can voice my deepest thoughts to. I do not believe he was dodging me on the afterlife question; I'm sure he has studied the matter in depth. He sized me up very quickly. So I am on a quest? Yes, that is a good word for my 'longing' for the unknown. Can a quest go on eternally? With that unsettling thought, we arrive at home.

I must prepare for the trip to Jerusalem a few days hence. We have extensive enterprises in Jerusalem and it is time for the yearly review.

+ + +

With Daniel, my cousin and my chief assistant, and three attendants we depart on the week's first day for Jerusalem. Our group includes Nahor, a slave, who drives the cart drawn by two donkeys and partially filled with wine and fresh vegetables for Uncle Levi. Philip and Nicolas are Phoenician free gentiles from Sidon. They are very good with numbers – for the inventory. They ride in the cart or walk, or both. Daniel and I are on our horses.

After a rather long while in silence, except for the Phoenicians chatting non-stop in Greek, Daniel asks, "Ethan, do you think we will get to Jerusalem before nightfall?"

"I think so. Why? Do you have plans for the evening?" My cousin Daniel is a little on the wild side, like my younger brother Caleb, and uses these trips to the city to sow even more wild oats. A family tradition I did not inherit.

"Oh, no. I was just wondering" as he looks away. With a playfully suspicious glance, he knows I've read his intentions correctly.

As for me, I will spend my time immersed in the business of our Jerusalem outlets with my Uncle Levi who oversees the chain of shops throughout the city. The economy has slowed down, due to the Roman tax increase in my opinion, and our sales are down for the year. Father has asked for a new business plan to deal with the reduced profits. I haven't come up with any ideas, probably because I am still preoccupied with the Scribe's claims about eternal life. Why can't I forget about this? The 'longing' has made it difficult to concentrate on business and made me melancholic. I am prone to melancholy. It's the mysterious 'longing'. I look forward to seeing Rabbi Asa soon.

We meet my friend Eli and his entourage returning to Ephraim. Eli is an old friend and an occasional fellow member of the Torah study group. "Ethan, good to see you! And you, Daniel."

"Did you have a profitable trip Eli?"

"Yes, but all work and no play. Oh, do you remember the Pharisee's talk on the afterlife?" Remember it? If he only knew.

"Yes, of course", I answer flatly.

"There is a rabbi from Galilee just up there around the next bend, and he is teaching a group in the olive grove about heaven and all that about eternal life. If he's still there you should stop and listen. He's a good speaker. I guess he is a Jew too." Eli has picked up the aggravating and spreading habit of calling all religious Israelites 'Jews'.

"Daniel" I ask as we move on, "are you a Jew?"

Daniel chuckles, "No, Ethan, I am not a Jude, or Jew. Jews are those from the tribe of Judah." This is an inside joke in the family about my insistence on historical correctness and Daniel has been through the exercise many times.

"Right, Daniel, we are Ephramites of the tribe of Ephraim, the sons of the saintly Joseph.

"Of course, we are all Jews to the Romans," says Daniel. End of exercise.

+ + +

After we part I hurry our group because I want to hear the Galilean teacher. We take a place to the rear of the mostly seated crowd. Daniel and I have a good view from our mounts.

Jesus, as someone addressed him, tells a story about a sinful tax collector being more justified before Yahweh than a Pharisee! This teacher definitely is not a Pharisee.

Jesus asks the women to bring their children to him for a blessing.

While he entertains the children, I take my impressions of this rabbi: He is of medium height with a pleasant but rather ordinary face covered with the traditional beard. He looks to be about my age, early thirties. What is striking is a strong, clear, gentle voice and piercing dark eyes. As he looks from child to child those eyes lock onto one child at a time, arresting their fidgeting and calming them immediately.

Jesus stands and addresses the adults: "Truly I say to you, whoever does not receive the kingdom of God like a child will not enter it at all."

This is strange teaching. I am drawn to stay and listen. Surely there are no answers here. This man is a Galilean peasant- I can spot them a mile away. What is he doing down here?   He has not acknowledged our presence, although the others in the crowd of about one hundred have glanced warily at us since we arrived. We are obviously of the ruling class (yes, they too can spot us a mile away). We are likely not the usual audience for this rabbi. His opinion about eternal life should be interesting.

I dismount, and the crowd parts before me as I confidently approach Jesus. His eyes meet mine steadily. He does not speak and shows no evidence of recognizing my superior standing. He smiles slightly which adds to a disarming and inviting presence. His gaze is captivating. Without a word as yet, I have his full attention. "Good Teacher, what shall I do to inherit eternal life?"

"Why do you call me good? No one is good except God alone." He pauses, as if knowing I need a moment to consider that startling statement. I was being polite in addressing him as 'good', but he took 'good' seriously. Maybe he is a Pharisee after all with that attention to detail. Is he mocking me, because I am a Sadducee? Suddenly, he says: "You know the commandments, "do not commit adultery, do not murder, do not steal, do not bear false witness, honor your father and mother."

"All these things I have kept from my youth", I answer truthfully. I had grown into my name: Ethan, the solid, enduring one, the good

9

steward. His eyes still fixed on mine, he shows no reaction to my reply.

"One thing you still lack: sell all that you possess and distribute it to the poor, and you shall have treasure in heaven; and come, follow Me."

I am confounded! Somehow my hope had risen that he might have answers about the longing. But sell all that I possess? The riches are not even legally mine yet. He could not know how complicated that would be. He could not know how many people depend on me. There are no answers here and I am mystified by the profound sadness that envelops me. Jesus is looking on me with compassion even as he delivers a second blow: "How hard it is for those who are wealthy to enter the kingdom of God! For it is easier for a camel to go through the eye of a needle than for a rich man to enter the kingdom of God." His words pierce my heart. My emotional state of sadness haunts me. Why do I care what this peasant says?

He turns away from me as someone asks, "Then who can be saved?" Jesus turns back.

"The things that are impossible with people are possible with God" he says without taking his eyes off of me, as if he were addressing me alone. He says no more. I sense I am being dismissed. In my sadness, not anger, I cannot muster a dutiful and polite farewell. I move back toward Nekoda and pause before mounting to look back. His eyes, those knowing eyes, are still fixed on me. The crowd is silent and every face looks confused, a mirror of my own disheartened countenance. Though they are not rich, I can see a look of compassion and solidarity with me as they too ponder his hard saying. In a few words this Jesus the Nazarene has turned upside down the belief that riches are the reward for righteousness. Jesus' gaze and the slightest nod seems to say that we will meet again.

+ + +

Rabbi Asa has arrived for his visit with Abba and the family. He and I will have our time together after lunch. In the few weeks since our meeting in Shiloh and my encounter with the Galilean Rabbi Jesus, I have thought of little else. I am eager to talk with Asa as he approaches.

"Rabbi Asa, I have been anxious awaiting this time with you."

"I too have looked forward to seeing you again."

I launch right in: "Asa, shortly after our first meeting, on a business trip to Jerusalem, I came upon a rabbi, a Galilean named Jesus. He was teaching in an olive grove to about a hundred people."

"That's quite a roadside crowd! I'm envious already." Asa's wit is never far away. "Tell me more!"

I recall all of the details of my encounter with Jesus. I am surprisingly able to precisely quote the words of Jesus I heard that day. Asa listens intently, without interrupting.

"Asa, I was strangely affected by this Rabbi Jesus. The words, the looks, Jesus' presence, are vivid in my memory. I cannot grasp his real intent. There must be a hidden meaning, for it would be irresponsible to literally sell all and follow him. Even if I wanted to, even if it would satisfy my longing, my quest, it would be selfish and ungrateful to my family and the workers who depend on me. But I sensed he had authority; that he was perhaps a prophet."

After a moments pause, Asa responds: "Ethan, I have heard of this intenerate rabbi. He is a Nazarene, yes, a Galilean as you surmised. There have been others like him in recent times; some have claimed they were the Messiah. All have faded away with time;

some of the more troublesome were jailed or executed. Beware of false prophets!

"Yes Asa, I have heard of these false prophets. We have discussed some of them in our Torah group. Their claims never intrigued me."

"But this one does?" Asa says.

"Yes, this one does intrigue me. He did not claim to be the Messiah, nor did he talk of eternal life, the afterlife. He seemed to be neither Sadducee or Pharisee. On reflection, he does not appear to respect boundaries.

"Boundaries?" Asa is puzzled.

I explain, "The Nazarene had an audience of peasants, both men and women, man and wife, sitting together. And small children, most running about causing a disturbance – until he kneeled before them and they became quiet as he blessed them. And us, the ruling class, when we arrived. Daniel and I were just one of the crowd, no different to him than the peasants. Jesus crossed all of our boundaries – no, the boundaries simply were not there."

"Asa, I remember as if it was happening now. The sour odor of the gathered peasants is still with me. The bright faces of the children are before me. Jesus' clear strong voice and those piercing eyes are embedded in me."

Asa responds seriously, "Ethan, you are vulnerable to clever preachers. Your quest demands that you reach out beyond traditional boundaries and therein lies many a snare."

"Snares? Clever preachers who are demon possessed?"

"We Sadducees do not believe in demons. I simply mean that when you have nursed a mysterious desire you can be highly susceptible to sirens."

"Like Homer's Odysseus?" I reply flatly. "I've read the Greeks. No, this is different – but I admit that I do not know how it is different."

Asa sighs and falls back into the chair. "I have this advice for you. Do not abandon the quest. Dig deeper into Israel's history and people. Tie a firm tether to the Torah, and especially to the Shema:

> *"Hear, O Israel! The LORD is our God, the LORD is one! You shall love the LORD your God with all your heart and with all your soul and with all your might. These words, which I am commanding you today, shall be on your heart."*

Asa pauses to carefully compose his direction.

"When you look within yourself, or listen to another for God's will, always test what you hear by the Torah, the Shema. What you find must confirm that God loves us, and that we shall love God and neighbor. If it does not, it is not from God."

"That is powerful direction. That is real wisdom. I thank you from the bottom of this questing heart." We embrace. Asa departs with "Until we meet again."

News arrives from Jerusalem. The Romans have crucified Jesus!

+ + +

A few days later, Daniel and I are inspecting improvements to the sheep and cattle pastures in the valley an hours walk from the villa. I need the exercise, and Nekoda dislikes short trips with a lot of starts and stops. It is a fine Spring day.

Cousin Daniel asks: "Ethan, why do you think the Romans executed Jesus? It has been on my mind always since hearing the news." My wild cousin Daniel has changed since our brief encounter with Jesus last harvest time. He mended his wayward ways, has been saying his prayers, and is a regular at the Synagogue. He has even joined the Torah study group. His change is somewhat mysterious. Daniel told the group that the words of Jesus that day have altered his view of life, but that he cannot explain it in a rational way. I am puzzled because he heard what I heard and there were no answers for me, even though I cannot put away the memory of Jesus the Nazarene. Daniel has changed, but has not shown any inclination to sell all and follow Jesus. We have not talked with each other about the changes Jesus apparently brought to both of us. I am very reluctant to discuss serious life matters with work associates even if they are family.

I decide to answer Daniel plainly: "Well, I have heard that the Sanhedrin found him guilty of blasphemy and convinced the Romans to crucify him because he might incite rioting among the Passover crowds." I knew this strait forward report is not what my now somewhat mystical cousin wants to hear. My reasoned account also belies my own strangely emotional response to the news of Jesus' crucifixion.

I continue, "But it has only been a couple of weeks; perhaps we will learn more when we return to Jerusalem." This was my way of telling Daniel that I really didn't want to talk about it. I wondered why I didn't, but I didn't. Daniel, sensing my discomfort, excused himself to go talk with the head herdsman who was approaching.

We had been eating lunch beneath one of the few trees in the sheep pasture in the valley below our estate home. It was the first warm day of early Spring, and the shade of the tree invited me to linger awhile - though I was already way behind in the day's tasks. We were consulting with the herdsman about some noxious weeds that were spreading and affecting the sheep. I will leave this matter to Daniel, because it is another one of those petty things that seem to bother me more and more. I linger in my thoughts. 'Why am I so resentful about my duties? Why has my melancholy and benign longing changed into resentment? This is an alarming change. If not corrected it will cripple my ability to be the manager and steward I am called to be. The encounter with Jesus is where it started. My sadness at his preposterous proposal quickly turned to anger, then resentment.

Why did I have such high expectations from this now dead rabbi? Why did I begin deeply examining what it is that he asked me to give up? My conclusions? Truly, I say, it is not the luxuries of wealth for myself, but my responsibilities to others that are binding. Duty, honor, and tradition, these three; and the greatest of these is duty. I really believe this, but something about it rings hollow, something is missing. But duty calls whether I resent it or not. There are no real options, no realistic choices for me. Happiness will come only if I stay the course appointed for me.

With self-directed encouragement I rise and stride with authority towards Daniel and the herdsmen who are now in a heated debate about the weeds. 'Vanity, vanity, all is vanity...Oh, Qoheleth where are you when I need you!'

I quickly settle the debate. "You will spend the next month digging up the weeds and burning them instead of just standing around and watching the sheep eat the damned weeds", I order the shepherds in my most forceful voice. I have long sought a way to make shepherds more productive. This may be a start. Daniel and I leave the shepherds to grumble - and get over it - they have no choices either. The day is about over. "Daniel, go by the south field on your way home and check on the water trenching progress. I'm going on back home." It has been another day of frustration and resentment. I despair in thinking that tomorrow will be no different. Oh, for a day to awake with excitement and anticipation of life again!

+ + +

The sounds of music and singing waft down from our villa in the grove. There is a party going on! What? On Thursday? There was no celebration scheduled for tonight.

"Simeon, what is going on?" I call to the chief house servant who has just come out into the back courtyard. Simeon turns and sprints the still considerable distance between me and home. Simeon is excited and breathless and shouts as he approaches,

"Your brother has come, and your father has killed the fattened calf because he has received him back safe and sound."

The resentment and anger that has been building in me overwhelms me. Simeon sees the anger burning in my eyes as I look with disbelief towards the villa. He shuffles, averts his eyes, and stammers out that Father had sent him out to get me so I could join the welcome for Caleb.

"Like hell I will welcome back that sorry, good for nothing scoundrel!" I thunder at Simeon. "You go and tell your Master that I will not come!" I realize I could not even call him Father, and certainly not Abba, so great is my anger. Simeon hesitates, for he knows wisdom sometimes follows anger.

"Go, Simeon, now!" He moves deliberately back towards the villa, despondent about being chosen messenger for this painful family divide.

I stand there, not knowing where to go. The sounds of laughing and singing wash over me as I just sit down on the path in utter frustration. I stare into the darkening valley, my back to the villa where the blasphemous music and singing persist. I barely see the shepherds in the dimming distance, still huddled and surely still complaining about their hard hearted master. But they are not unlike me, whose own master, whose own Father has turned away from a faithful and dutiful son to embrace a traitorous son, my own brother. I sit staring at the distant shepherds, with tears welling up from my sense of betrayal. I have no idea of what to do next. So I sit, paralyzed in my fury.

"Ethan?" comes my Father's voice from behind, hesitant and inquiring. "Caleb has returned. Please come in and welcome him." I remain silent, still looking toward the shepherds who have disappeared in the twilight. After what seems to be a long silence, Father sits beside me.

"Ethan, I know what you are thinking. We both know what a stupid and terrible thing Caleb has done. There is no excusing his selfishness and his sins. But he is truly sorry. When I saw him coming and ran out to him, Caleb spoke first and confessed his sin and unworthiness", Father pauses and looks to me for a response. I have none. "Ethan, forgiveness should always be the favored sentence of judgment, surely with a brother." Now he lectures me! "Caleb is guilty but repentant. Forgive him and come in and welcome him." Is he pleading with me or commanding me?

I cannot contain my anger and indignation. "Look! For so many years I have been serving you and I have never neglected a command of yours; and yet you have never given me a young goat, so that I might celebrate with my friends; but when this son of yours came, who has devoured your wealth with prostitutes, you killed the fattened calf for him." Immediately after this spontaneous outburst, I realize that jealousy also, not just righteous indignation, is a cause of my anger and frustration. I had never thought I had even the capacity for jealousy, certainly not of Caleb Stephanas bar Phinehas, my little brother. But jealousy was a part of it. I come to a stark realization that I do not know myself - I do not know who I am. I am standing at a great abyss, with no choice but to leap into the darkness. My Father sensed the profound struggle going on inside me. In a curiously matter of fact way, he simply said:

"Son, you have always been with me, and all that is mine is yours. But we have to celebrate and rejoice, for this brother of yours was dead and has begun to live, and was lost and has been found." Then he got up and returned to the party to leave me alone with my struggles.

'For this brother of yours was dead and now has begun to live, and was lost and has been found.' The words of my Father burned into my soul. 'And now I am dead and lost' I say out loud to myself. 'And to where do I return? What do I confess? Who do I confess to?' My stupid young brother is in a better place than I am. The abyss is shrouded with questions, with no assurance that a plunge into the darkness will be cushioned by answers. Without deliberately choosing, I seem to descend into the darkness of the abyss, even as the darkness of night descends upon me. And the party goes on - without further pleading for me to join in. There is a conspiracy of silence and solitude that allows me to struggle with myself - and with God. There must be answers about life beyond duty, honor, and tradition. Where might they lie? Only one ever suggested to me that there may be another way. Jesus of Nazareth. His words come back to me: "One thing you still lack; sell all that you possess and distribute it to the poor, and you shall have treasure in heaven; and come, follow me." And I remember my question: "Good Teacher, what shall I do to inherit eternal life?" If he truly was a prophet, or even the Messiah as some say, could that brief meeting have been a message from God, to me, Ethan, just for this time? I remember how his eyes were so fixed on mine, as if he were talking only to me, not the crowd around him. He may have been a prophet. He certainly is not the Messiah, for now he is dead.

By the now risen moon and dew around me I realize that I have been sitting here for hours. The party goes on without me. The songs are all very familiar, but I have no desire for the familiar. I recall a Psalm we discussed at the Torah group:

I waited patiently for the LORD;
And He inclined to me and heard my cry.
He brought me up out of the pit of destruction, out of the miry
clay,
And He set my feet upon a rock making my footsteps firm.
He put a new song in my mouth,

Is there a new song for me? Is there a rock to make my footsteps firm?

Ending my contemplation, I cannot resist the desire to look in on the 'party'. I go in through the servants entry. I do not wish to be seen. Through the entry hall that opens to the courtyard festivities I can see the celebrating party. I slip up behind two servants and motion them to be still. As I see Caleb dancing with our sister Sherah, I realize that the impassioned anger toward Caleb – and Father – still grips me. I slip away to my rooms for a fitful night – a dark night for my soul.

+ + +

There is no family breakfast today. The revelers need sleep more than food. Simeon returns with Caleb's reply: "Master Ethan, Caleb sends his greetings and agrees to meet with you at the olive grove at the fourth hour," he says in his formal voice.

"Thank you Simeon. See that we are not disturbed."

"Yes sir." I believe Simeon actually relishes this family fight and disguises his feelings with formality.

The stone and olive wood benches at the edge of the grove invite a pleasant meeting of friends – not at all what will take place in a few minutes.

"Good morning Ethan." Caleb is visibly afraid of what may happen next. He does not offer his hand, relieving me of the insult of refusing it. He waits for my move with fear in his darting eyes.

"Caleb, why did you do it?" hiding my anger behind fixed eyes.

"Master Ethan…"

"Stop it!" I almost shout. "I am your brother!" No point in trying to hide my anger.

"My elder brother – and my master." He is accepting that I am on higher ground.

My anger rising, I demand, "You are avoiding the question! It is simple: Why did you do it?"

"Frustration, desire, adventure" Caleb's opening is rehearsed. He adds, "All growing from my selfishness and stupidity, as I learned later." Caleb's fear has receded as he begins a confession that he has thought about and lived with a long time.

"Let's take those one at a time" I say. Despite the anger, I find myself turning to my analytical self. "Frustration?" I assume his answer will be that of the second son pattern– a myth in my opinion.

Caleb begins his rational litany. "Frustration. First, not envy of your position. I do not have the personality nor the gifts for stewarding the estate of Phinehas bar Ezer. All of us know that. But life as a son of any standing in this rich, formal family seemed suffocating to me then. Ethan, I was nineteen…"

"Stop again! Age is no excuse! I am unaware of any other minority sons who did what you did at nineteen!" This in my most demanding voice.

"You are right", Caleb says meekly. "I could not see a good life before me. The riches have never been important to me." He knew this is not news to me.

"Desire is next" I say expectantly.

Caleb shifts and looks away. "In a word: sex." That I can understand and decide to move on.

"Adventure?" I want to point out that being rich affords adventures aplenty, but decide to let him answer.

"Ethan, I am now 22 years and you are 33 years. Have you ever been on a real adventure unaccompanied by family and servants? Will you ever?" Caleb is getting bold, and I am getting calmer. He continues, "I wanted, and still want, to see the wider world. Not just Rome, Athens, Alexandra. What is to the far east? I want to know." Caleb pauses but not long enough for my retort. "Or I could have a nominal family position while actually being a roving, fornicating, pretend Prince living off your wealth. I tried that and I honestly don't want that."

"What do you want, Caleb?" I am surprised with the touch of empathy in my voice.

"This will shock you, but I have had a lot of time and experiences to think about that. I just want to help people who need help, and even to help them be happy."

But it does not shock me. Caleb has always been a gentle soul, quick to defer to others. Mother, in scolding Caleb for one of his playful pranks, would often say "Caleb, you have the mind of a peasant." It seemed never to occur to him that his friends should be among our class. He was not rebellious (until he was!); such discrimination just was not in his blood, though I cannot imagine why not!

Caleb continues, "I never knew there was so much suffering and poverty in the world of the slaves and peasants. Then I myself fell to the poorest of the poor. I lived their suffering. I know you will say that I did not have to experience it to believe it, but I'm not so sure. I am not justifying the crimes - sins – I committed against family and God. There must be a better way to come to the belief that I choose to live for others, but I am not aware of a better way."

This is not going as I had imagined. It is going much better. My anger has evaporated as if swept away by the sudden gust of wind that came up a few moments ago. Caleb is truly repentant, I can see that. He also is grasping for a way to devote his life to others from within the family. I believe we have begun a real reconciliation.

"Caleb, this has been a good talk. I appreciate your honesty and frankness. I believe we are on the right path."

"Dear Brother Ethan, I have always looked up to you. You could not have been a better brother to grow up with. I love you, my brother."

I offer my hand –but not yet an embrace. "See you later."

+ + +

It has been several days since confronting Caleb. Abba, in his way, assumes that we have reconciled fully. He is the consummate optimist. I do not believe I have really forgiven Caleb, or for that matter, Abba either. However, the tension is easing with time. We are back to our duties and things appear normal. I do often wonder how things would be if Mother were here. She will not return from her family home in Tyre for several weeks yet, unless she cuts short her visit when she receives news of Caleb's return. I suspect that will be the case.

As my focus on Caleb ebbs, I return to the mystery of the Nazarene's hold on my thoughts. My deep despair has eased, giving way to hope, I hope. The reports about Jesus are increasing. There are rumors about Jesus being the Messiah since he has a growing following even after his death. There are reports by people who claim to be eye witnesses who say they saw him dead and then alive again in a few days. The most intriguing report is that Joseph, my friend in Arimathea secured a tomb and buried Jesus. I can trust my friend from childhood for the truth.

I send a message to Rabbi Asa that I am undertaking a quest. I shall go to Arimathea to see Joseph to inquire about this. And I shall go to Jerusalem to seek out these disciples of Jesus who are causing a stir about his resurrection. There is one Simon from Galilee that I have heard about. They say Jesus called him Peter - the rock. Yes, at dawn I will go to see Joseph, and this man called Peter.

The journey to Arimathea gives me ample time to reflect on the events of the past few days. Nekoda was a gift to my Father from the Roman Legatus Legionis commanding the Legion responsible for peace in Ephraim. Peace, of course, is defined by the Romans: Pax Romano! That means pacification of an area and prompt collection of taxes due. It is a forced peace, but in Ephraim the pax had not turned to a pox, largely due to Abba's leadership. Cooperation with the Romans is realistic and practical. Phinehas bar Ezer takes a rather benign view of the Roman occupation. Such has happened many times in our history and this too shall pass. Religious ideology, such as that of the Zealots, was useless and especially harmful to the peasants in my Father's view. It never occurred to me to challenge Abba's policy.

It is the first time I can remember traveling a distance without at least two or three servants, and although I never considered their presence confining, I now realized how little time I had ever spent in solitude. I remember Jesus saying how hard it was for a rich man to enter the kingdom of heaven. Perhaps solitude is a good thing - and a rich man has little time for solitude. I have had little else for the past two days. My meditations have been anguishing. There was a connection between Jesus' words to me - *"One thing you still lack; sell all that you possess and distribute it to the poor, and you shall have treasure in heaven; and come, follow Me"* - and my raging anger over my Father's welcome of my once lost brother. I have come to no resolution of these seemingly unconnected events, and it continues to haunt me. One thing I know, I cannot go on as before. I can no longer believe that life is predestined according to your birthright and family position. There is something beyond tradition, honor, and duty. Even my sorry brother Caleb must have understood that. I have not forgiven him - or my Father. The anger begins to overtake the hope that had spurred me on this quest for truth.

As Nekoda continues his steady pace, I begin to think of the long history of our family and the land in which we live. The hill country of our ancestors was named after Ephraim, the second born of Joseph in Egypt. Joseph's father Jacob, now Israel, as he was dying took Ephraim and his older brother Manasseh to bless them. Then Jacob, whose eyesight was very weak, blessed Ephraim first and Manasseh second over the objections of Joseph. But Jacob would not relent and said Ephraim would be the greater although Manasseh would also be the father of a great people.

When Joshua assigned the lands of Canaan to the tribes, the tribe of Ephraim received as its inheritance the rich hill country north of Jerusalem and in the center of Israel. The tribe of Manasseh received lands which are now Samaria and other lands in the Golan heights. Why did Jacob switch the blessings of Ephraim and Manasseh? Was he consciously repeating his Father Isaac's mistake when Jacob deceived him and received the blessing that should have gone to Esau? Was Isaac's choice really a mistake? Was Jacob's? My Father's decision to give Caleb a large part of his inheritance before bestowing the same on me seems to continue this history of confused inheritances. While I was not displaced as the elder son by his actions, it was definitely a break with tradition to grant Caleb an inheritance before his time. I don't think I will ever understand Abba's reasoning. But somehow the anger has faded.

The sight of the lush, almost tropical oasis of Joseph's estate in Arimathea arrested the anger and renewed the hope. I have known

Joseph since childhood, for his family ruled this area about halfway to the Great Sea, as my family did in Ephraim. The approach was a long road lined with towering palms and the heat of the desert-like low hill country dissipated as I rode into the gardens surrounding the expansive estate home. The smell of sweet shrub was in the spring time air; the yellow and red of the alamander and oleander were brilliant against the terra cotta walls. Two servants, an old married couple, Moesha and Rebekah, hurry towards me, welcoming me respectfully, and obviously happy to see me. They have known me since I was very young.

"Master Ethan, we are so happy to see you."

"It is so good to see you two looking so healthy and happy! It has been more than a year since my last visit. Too long."

"Master, Master Joseph is not here and we are worried" Moesha said immediately. "Let us get you settled and refreshed and we would like to share with you our worries, if you will allow."

"Of course", I reply, joining them in mutual worry. After a time of refreshment in the cool of the reception room, Moesha and Rebekah rejoin me.

"Master Joseph left for Jerusalem several weeks ago for a Sanhedrin Council meeting. He said it was about another false prophet causing trouble. He was to return within the week. But there was trouble in Jerusalem and we have heard a report of the crucifixion of a rabbi from Nazareth - Jesus - we think this is the one Master Joseph was called about." Moesha is talking excitedly and Rebekah is nervous at his lack of decorum. I interrupt: "I have heard these reports also, Moesha; but have you not heard from Joseph?"

"No", replies Moesha gravely, "but some people from down at Emmaus came and told us there is much trouble in Jerusalem because the disciples of this Jesus say he is alive again after dying on the cross."

"Rebekah, what else did the folks from Emmaus have to say?"

With my permission to speak, Rebekah responds haltingly, "They said that they heard that our Master Joseph took Jesus' body and bought a burial cave near Golgotha and buried Jesus. And he is now hiding from the Council since they believe he is also a disciple of Jesus. How can this be so, Master Ethan?"

"I don't believe this can be so, Rebekah", I say unconvincingly. "Are these people of Emmaus reliable?"

"They are servants like us. They have been our friends for a long time and we have always believed them to be truthful." Moesha is calmer now. "But, Master Ethan, they claim to have spoken with Jesus after his crucifixion when they were returning to Emmaus from Jerusalem. They are among those spreading the rumor of Jesus' resurrection. Does this not make them unreliable? Perhaps they have lost their minds and their report that Master Joseph is in danger is also not true." Moesha pauses.

"But then, where is he?" Rebekah asks searchingly.

"Moesha, Rebekah, I shall go to Jerusalem and see and I will send word. You are not to worry any more until you hear from me." I realize my command not to worry is nonsense, but I am trained to believe that servants obey whatever I say - and they do have hopeful smiles now that someone with authority will do something.

+ + +

Jerusalem is bustling as usual, but there is a noticeable tension in the air of the central market area. Roman contubeniums with 8 soldiers are stationed at key intersections. They are in full battle regalia even to the trademark plume of feathers on their bronze helmets. They do not intend to go unnoticed.

There are more than the usual groups of older men talking quietly and casting furtive and suspicious glances at passersby, like me. As I reach my uncle's office , Roman troops shout me aside as they move double time toward some disturbance beyond a walled courtyard and out of view.

"Ethan" my uncle Levi calls out. "I did not expect you. This is not a good time for business in Jerusalem." Uncle Levi is a large and robust man, my Father's youngest brother. Only ten years my senior, he is a good friend as well as my uncle. "I'm here on personal business, Levi." I choose not to go into the details of my recent experiences; the news of Caleb's return probably had not reached him. I go right to the point.

"Levi, I am searching for Joseph from Arimathea. His people believe he is in trouble."

"Yes Ethan, I have heard the rumors about him being in with the Galileans. The Romans crucified their rabbi, one Jesus of Nazareth. There are rumors that he has come alive from the dead. Of course someone has stolen the body. The Sanhedrin believes this is a plot by the Zealots and is pushing for the arrest of the rabbi's followers. Joseph is a member of the Council - how could he be allied with the Galileans?"

"I must find Joseph." Levi sees my deep concern.

"Ethan, you live a sheltered life in Ephraim. I live here in the heart of Jerusalem, and there is always trouble in Jerusalem. This too shall pass."

"That does not mean that Joseph is not in danger", I answer pointedly. "Do you know where Joseph might be?"

Levi answers, "I have inquired and was told he might be at a house near the Essene Gate, but my men were turned away. Things are tense, people aren't talking much."

I arrive at the house near the Essene Gate where Levi had made inquiries about Joseph. After a long time of persistent knocking, the door is opened by an earnest and worried young man. "I am Ethan of Ephraim and am looking for my friend Joseph of Arimathea. I mean no harm to anyone, I am just concerned for my dear friend" trying to voice the same earnestness that my greeter's countenance portrays. "His family is very worried about him", I venture on as he looks at me without replying. Searching for a connection, I offer falsely, "I was told to ask for the man called Peter." I am surprised when he motions me inside, still without speaking.

Finally, he speaks, "Wait here" he says and disappears down a long hallway.

"Ethan, what a joy to see an old friend!" Joseph hugs me before I can respond, surprised by my good fortune.

"Joseph, thank the Lord you are safe." We are immediately reunited in a brotherhood reserved only for childhood friends. "Joseph, I've heard all sorts of bizarre tales about the rabbi from Nazareth and about you burying him and being his disciple and..." Joseph stops me. "Come sit and I'll tell you an amazing story. Amazing but true." Joseph is serious but joyful.

I am stunned by Joseph's story. He had become a secret disciple of Jesus, along with our mutual friend Nicodemus, after a night time meeting with Jesus. When Jesus was condemned to death they requested the Romans' permission to bury Jesus. The Romans, he said, were glad to finally get even the dead Jesus off their hands. After buying a burial cave Joseph laid Jesus to rest. The Romans came and sealed the cave with a large boulder and posted guards to prevent the Zealots from stealing the body. When the women came on Sunday, the boulder had been rolled back and the tomb was empty. Then Jesus actually appeared to the women and later to all of his disciples. Joseph was with the other disciples when Jesus appeared and ate fish to show the doubters that he was really alive. Joseph was very convincing because he did not seem to realize how incredible his story was. I am full of questions when he finally pauses.

"How do you know he was really dead?"

"Ethan, I carried him to the tomb. Nicodemus and I were hours preparing the body for burial. Jesus had bled a lot from the piercing of his wrists and feet and a stab wound in his side." Joseph is choking with tears as he relives the gruesome task of the burial. "He was dead, Ethan" he says with a determined finality.

"You actually saw Jesus alive later - you personally?" My doubts are logical to me.

"Yes, Ethan, personally." Joseph has become formal and I realize he has assumed a forensic attitude in keeping with his training as a lawyer and a member of the Council. He knew he was being cross examined as in a courtroom. His earnest telling of the events confirms my appreciation that this man was not just an old childhood friend but a highly intelligent and skilled ruler of his people. I am convinced that he is telling the truth.

It was then my time to tell Joseph my story of the haunting memory of my encounter with Jesus months earlier. Of that encounter which turned my indefinite longing into a desperate desire for real meaning in life. And how that frustrated desire had turned to anger as I accepted my fate as if I had no choices. And how that anger erupted when my Father joyfully and graciously welcomed back his lost son - my sorry brother Caleb. And how the calm after that angry storm left me aimless - about who I was or where I was to go. And the urge to seek out the only one who ever offered me a choice - Jesus of Nazareth – now a dead man. And to seek out Joseph and Peter. And now the news that he is dead no longer. As I conclude, Joseph must sense my hopeful yet unconvinced heart.

"Ethan, I do not understand how, but I believe that Jesus is the answer. Simon, the man Jesus called Peter, is in the upper room here with other disciples since Jesus was taken up to heaven ten days ago. We have gathered in prayer as Jesus told us to. He said to wait in Jerusalem and pray until the Father baptized us with the Holy Spirit. We do not know what that really means, but perhaps this power of the Holy Spirit is for you also. Come, follow me." I follow him.

We enter the sparsely furnished upper room crowded with perhaps a hundred people. Some are prostrate in prayer, others are sitting or standing silently like strangers waiting to be introduced. One man stands at a window looking at the now busy street below. I sit beside Joseph as he closes his eyes and begins a soft murmuring prayer. I begin to meditate on this bizarre journey. Without knowing how, I realize I have put all my hope toward a belief that Jesus is really alive from the dead and is the Messiah – long foretold and promised in Scripture- God with us. I find myself praying that the power of the holy spirit that Joseph spoke of will empower me to know Jesus and myself, that I may have a special destiny and the will to fulfill it.

Suddenly, a loud noise like the wind of a fierce storm startles our gathering. I look out the small window above, but the sky is clear. What is that noise that is literally shaking the room? Before any of us can move, flickers of light, like fireflies, fill the room. What appears to be sparks of fire are falling from the ceiling. What is happening? There is great confusion and shouting but no one is trying to leave. I am confused and bewildered. How can this be? I stand in awestruck silence for what seems to be a long time. I seem to be suspended in a trance as the excitement and commotion of the room goes on around me, but somehow apart from me. As suddenly as it came my confusion melts away and I am overcome with a sense of peace that passes my understanding. A feeling of blessed warmth engulfs me and a glow comes up from within me like that of the now invisible tongues of fire that had filled the room. I know, in some new way of knowing, that the glow and warmth and peace in me is really Jesus. He is risen indeed! Suddenly, no longer in my suspended state, I too am embracing Joseph and others with shouts of "Praise the Lord, Praise the Lord!"

Joseph points to several men who have gathered at the front of the room. "They are the twelve that Jesus called the Apostles. There is Simon Peter" he points out the man speaking quietly to the group. Finally the excitement subsides somewhat and someone asks "What does this mean?" Others pick up the question, "Yes, what does this mean?"

"It means you're drunk" shouts one of a group who have come in from outside to see what the commotion is about. "Yes", mocks another, "they are full of sweet wine!"

Simon rises to speak and immediately gets the attention he requests. Before this man called Peter speaks I know I am about to hear the truth about what all this means. Like my young brother, I know I was lost but now am found, was dead but now am about to live anew. Praise the Lord indeed!

+ + +

That strangely wonderful morning in the upper room near the Essene Gate had left me peaceful and contented. Content despite not having a plan for what to do next, very uncharacteristic for me the planner and manager. Within the few days that had passed, all of us there had been baptized by Peter and the twelve. Jesus' inner circle was still called the twelve even though one of them, Judas Iscariot, our Lord's betrayer had committed suicide. Great crowds had come to hear the twelve tell of Jesus the Messiah's death and resurrection and urging repentance and baptism of the Holy Spirit. Someone has said that over three thousand have already been baptized.

My stewarding personality begins to overtake my contentment as I ponder what I should do next. Many of Jesus early followers are coming together to await his return, which they believe is imminent. They are selling their possessions, which are few - basically what they carry with them - and going from house to house spreading the good news. Joseph, Nicodemus, and I have a little more complicated situation and the three of us discussed this last night. We all share a deep desire to worship and follow our Lord Jesus. We agree that we will indeed give all our possessions away if that is what Holy Spirit desires. But we all share a reluctance to make a quick decision without further guidance. The practical dimensions of life keep intruding on our spiritual desires. We are all sons of wealthy ruling families - Joseph of Arimathea, Nicodemus of a prominent Pharisee family in Hebron, and my family in Ephraim. Giving away our possessions is not very practical, and certainly not something we could do without the consent of others and without some legal actions.

We decide to ask Matthew, one of the twelve, for some guidance. Matthew had been a tax collector and therefore a man accustomed to wealth, unlike the rest of the twelve. I had not met Matthew but Joseph and Nicodemus had come to know him.

Matthew meets us in the same room I first entered at the house of the upper room. Matthew is older than the others of the twelve, with a somewhat stern countenance. But he greets me with a warm smile and an embrace when Joseph introduces us. Joseph gets right to the point.

"Matthew, we are in need of some direction about what we are to do. We all want to follow our Lord and do whatever He would want us to do. You know our families and our situations. Should we do what the others are doing, contribute all we have to the group and await our Lord's return?" Matthew does not answer immediately, but carefully studies the faces of the three rich young men before him.

"Matthew", I interrupt before he can reply, "can I tell you about my meeting Jesus before his crucifixion?" He nods, still not having spoken. I tell him about my encounter with Jesus on the road to Jerusalem, about my question of eternal life and Jesus' then shocking response to sell all I had, give it to the poor, and follow him; precisely the issue that we three face now. Only I face it for the second time. "Matthew, I am deeply troubled about not obeying Jesus and now about the temptation to repeat the disobedience." I am surprised at the smile that comes to his thus far stern and serious face.

"Ethan, your confession has shown me the way to help you, all of you." Matthew now appears confident and speaks with the authority that has mysteriously veiled the twelve since that day of the Holy Spirit in the upper room. "We must always remember the grace and mercy of our Lord. Ethan, your disobedience is only an example of a long history of disobedience by our people. Yet, despite being the sons of disobedience, the God of grace and mercy has come among us in Jesus our Lord, has died for our sins, and has risen to assure us of eternal life. This is the true love of God for us." Matthew grasps my hands in his, "Ethan, your confession is sincere, your sins are forgiven. Can you accept the love, grace, and mercy of our Lord?"

"I accept it."

"Bless you, my son. Now let us get on to where you three belong in the Kingdom of our Lord Jesus." Joseph and Nicodemus remain silent and seem somewhat amazed at this turn of events.

Matthew continues, "There are many among us who believe the Lord will return very soon. I hope so. But I cannot forget our risen Lord's words when he appeared to us in Galilee:

'Go therefore and make disciples of all the nations, baptizing them in the name of the Father and the Son and the Holy Spirit, teaching them to observe all that I commanded you; and lo, I am with you always, even to the end of the age.' Just before he ascended he also said: 'It is not for you to know times or epochs which the Father has fixed by His own authority; but you will receive power when the Holy Spirit has come upon you; and you shall be My witnesses both in Jerusalem, and in all Judea and Samaria, and even to the remotest part of the earth.' I had heard many of Jesus' sayings in the past few days, but not these.

"How can we make disciples of other nations if we stay here in Jerusalem waiting for his return?" Matthew asks rhetorically, thinking out loud to himself. "Perhaps we are not all called to do the same. Perhaps some are called to cloister themselves and pray and others to go out and proclaim the good news and make disciples." Matthew is clearly still in the process of thinking this through. He confirms this with "I have not talked to Peter or the other Apostles about this, but I shall give you some direction. If it is unwise, may the Lord have mercy once again."

"Jerusalem, Judea, Samaria, the world" Matthew continues his out loud thinking. Having reached some conclusion, Matthew confidently turns to speak to us, "We have many witnesses here in Jerusalem and the numbers are growing by the hour. You three live in the rest of Judea, you Joseph in Arimathea to the west, you Nicodemus in Hebron to the South, and you Ethan in Ephraim to the north. Who better to be the Lord's witnesses in Judea? I believe that God has chosen you for just this mission. Even your wealth and ruling position can be an advantage if dedicated to making disciples."

A troubling recollection comes to my mind, "Matthew, when I met Jesus that day he also said that it is easier for a camel to go through the eye of a needle than for a rich man to enter the kingdom of God."

Matthew astounds me with a quick and firm reply, "Ethan, I was there. Jesus also said 'the things that are impossible with people are possible with God'; and as I recall he was looking straight at you. Do you remember?" "Yes," I mutter , wondering if this Messiah was already shaping my destiny.

"Ethan - and Joseph and Nicodemus - pray that you really accept God's forgiveness and be troubled no more with feelings of guilt about your past or your present privileged positions. God has ordered this for his glory." Matthew now speaks with assurance and authority. "As an Apostle of Jesus Christ, I direct you to go back to your homes and bear witness to our Lord. Pray constantly to Holy Spirit who now indwells you for guidance in your actions from this day forward. I do not know what God has for you to do, but go now as God's chosen camels and seek the needle with full assurance that Holy Spirit will guide you through the eye into the fullness of the kingdom of God." Matthew's use of Jesus' simile seals the sacrament of the present moment.

With hugs and holy kisses Matthew leaves us. After some futile attempts to analyze what just happened with Matthew, Nicodemus suggests we just thank God for his love and grace and depart to our homes trusting that God will lead us by the right path.

+ + +

The solitary ride to Ephraim on my good horse Nekoda is a time of prayer and reflection. As I near the greening hills of home in the fading daylight of early summer, one thing becomes clear. Just as the Lord has forgiven me for my sins of disobedience, I must forgive the sins of my brother Caleb. The anger and contempt I had for Caleb had taken deep root in my soul. It is still there, but now desperately calling to be excised and cast away. I was not sure how to forgive him. Father seemed to forgive him spontaneously, letting his love simply drown out his judgment against Caleb that I knew he held. My desire to forgive Caleb seems more obligatory than loving, and this troubles me. And I must apologize to Father for my anger at his love for his own son! I would normally approach this tense family situation with anxiety, but now I am eager to heal the wounds. I believe the Lord will be with me and guide me if my heart truly seeks reconciliation. I pray that it does.

As I come within sight of our house I see Simeon, the chief house servant, dart inside to announce my coming. Immediately, my Father comes running out to meet me. "Come down off that stallion and give me a hug", he commands joyfully. "Welcome home. We heard from Levi about the trouble and you getting mixed up in it. I'm glad you are safe." I had not seen my uncle Levi since I first arrived in Jerusalem, but he had extensive contacts and apparently knew I had found Joseph - and the followers of Jesus. As we walked toward the villa the lingering estrangement from my brother pressed upon me.

"Abba, where is Caleb?"

My Father had not mentioned Caleb or my outburst at his return. "He has gone hunting with Daniel. They said they will be back tomorrow. I hope you want to see him." My Father glances at me expectantly.

"Yes, I do. Father, can we talk after I clean up and have some supper?"

"Yes Ethan, take your time."

+ + +

Father has a remarkable way of understanding by putting himself into the place of the other. In our talk last night, he had understood immediately that my anger at the return of Caleb was not out of disrespect towards him nor even really about my hatred toward Caleb. He had recognized my own inner struggle for purpose and meaning long before this. He called it the middle age crisis. He even shared some of his own middle age troubles. Father had listened politely about my Jerusalem adventure and my profession of being a baptized disciple of Jesus the Nazarene. He was respectful of our Israelite traditions and believed in Yahweh and said his prayers sporadically. But he was not a religious man. I could almost hear him thinking, 'and this too shall pass.' He wanted only the reconciliation of his sons.

He had some wise words about forgiveness. Frustration, he said, comes when we do not get our way. If we are self centered, our way is the only way that really matters, and the frustration becomes anger toward another. If we freeze that anger, in time it becomes hatred. When one hates, he cannot see the other person except in that past time. Forgiveness can come only when we release the past time and look at the person for who they are now. My Father had given me the way to fully reconcile with Caleb.

Caleb and cousin Daniel return in the heat of the afternoon loaded with freshly killed game - grouse and quail and three fat rabbits.

Caleb and I go down to the same meadow where I had sat paralyzed by anger and where our first encounter after his return took place. Neither of us speaks as we walk. I hope that we will complete the reconciliation that ended only in a handshake before.

To my surprise, the words of forgiveness and asking for his pardon come easily, for the forgiveness and desire for reconciliation were already in my heart. This is a new experience for me. The words seem to come from somewhere other than a previously thought out script. Caleb talks a little about his derelict journey and is sincerely repentant. We find ourselves talking easily and truly experiencing the joy of the present moment of reunion, the past fading into its non-existent state. As I try to think of a good way to tell of my Jerusalem experience, our talk takes a surprising turn.

"Ethan, on our hunting trip Daniel told me about the rabbi from Galilee, Jesus of Nazareth. Daniel says he is a disciple of Jesus. He believes he is the Messiah promised in the Scriptures. Have you heard about these things?" Caleb is serious; I am stunned!

I hastily begin to tell my story and Caleb interrupts. "Wait! Let's go get Daniel!"

When Daniel joins us I now calmly tell of my journey in search of our friend Joseph and how that led to the baptism of the Holy Spirit in the upper room. I tell of my conviction that Jesus is indeed the Messiah, now the risen Messiah who has died that we may have eternal life. I tell joyfully of the new song in my heart as I follow the direction of the Apostle Matthew.

"Matthew directed Joseph, Nicodemus, and me to return to our homes and tell of the good news of Jesus the Messiah. Thank God it begins here with my own family!"

"Ethan", Daniel begins excitedly, "you know that I was moved by Jesus when you talked to him that day on the road to Jerusalem. Jesus has disciples here in Ephraim and I have heard the stories of his healings and miracles. I believe that Jesus is the Messiah. But how can I be baptized by the Holy Spirit?"

"I want to be baptized too!" Caleb says, his beaming smile wider than ever. I had not thought about that.

"Go to Jerusalem and seek out the Apostles, some call them the twelve. There is Matthew, John, Andrew, James, Thaddaeus - I can't remember them all. Ask for the man called Peter - that got me in." I give them directions to the house of the upper room by the Essene Gate. They plan to leave in the morning.

I am alone again, sitting in the very same place in the meadow where I sat blind and lost in my anger and selfishness upon my brother's return. My Father's words that night come back to me: "... for this brother of yours was dead and now has begun to live, and was lost and has been found." 'Yes, Father, but there are two sons who were dead and have begun to live; two sons who were lost and have been found.'

+ + +

PART TWO

The ethereal shape of a man emerges through the heat waves disturbing the long views in the hot Ephraim summer. The long straight road to our villa is bordered by alternating palms and crepe myrtles, now in full bloom. The road serves a dual purpose. It's white marbled elegance announce the approach to an abode of distinction. It also announces to those who may have less than friendly intent that it was well guarded. Several of the men servants serve as guards in addition to their other duties. The Centurion at the Roman fortress near old Shechem provided the training and arms as a favor to my Father. Their presence is a constant reminder that all is not well in Palestine.

My Father Phinehas and I are reclining on the veranda after the light midday meal of yoghurt and honey, figs, dates, and blueberries - perfect for this uncomfortably hot afternoon. I motion toward the approaching apparition. We watch in silence as the ghost becomes incarnate on the hot white marbled road. Simeon, who is attending us, has already alerted the guard servant who comes to the veranda. The lone, now solid man is unarmed and poses no threat, so I dismiss the servants. What is my Father, still silent, thinking at this moment? Surely of that day when the approaching figure was Caleb. At what point on the long road home did he recognize the bedraggled Caleb and run out to embrace him? Have I really forgiven Caleb – and my Father, my Abba? I hope so.

The young man, moments ago inchoate in the white heat, is now whole and recognizable. He is one of the twelve! I saw him occasionally in Jerusalem – and he was in the upper room that day. But I was never introduced to him. I seem to remember him as always in the background, on the periphery of gatherings. I do not remember him ever speaking. But he is one of the twelve. He speaks now:

"Hello sirs, is this the home of Phinehas, ruler of Ephraim?" Does he recognize me? He has a low, hesitant Galilean peasant voice. "And sir" he fixes his squinting eyes on mine, "I know you are Ethan bar Phinehas who was with us in the upper room."

Abba draws the apostle's attention: "Yes, I am Phinehas. And who might you be?"

"Kind sir, I am Labbaeus Thaddaeus bar Alphaeus of Galilee, apostle of Jesus of Nazareth, the Messiah." He speaks in a forced, rehearsed manner failing to disguise a peculiar Aramaic dialect. Abba is taken aback by this peasant as he adds 'apostle of Jesus of Nazareth, the Messiah' to his formal introduction. Not a proper way to introduce yourself to one of the ruling class! Abba does not pursue his lineage since it is likely of no importance, him being from Galilee. Rather Abba defers to me, curious about how I will handle this delicate matter of the messiah. Abba knows of my profession that Jesus of Nazareth is the long awaited messiah, but we have not as yet discussed my 'situation'.

"Yes Labbaeus Thaddaeus, I am Ethan and we were together in Jerusalem. I regret we did not have the opportunity to meet personally. I do know you are one of the twelve." At that he seemed to relax a bit and his face seemed comforted. I moved down the steps to be with him, on the same level. Abba did not, of course. Abba seemed to accept the change in status from leader to curious bystander. My descent from the authoritative heights of the veranda somehow struck me as profound.

I looked back at my Father on high, standing tall and confident as one of high rank. Then I looked at Labbaeus Thaddaeus, an unimposing peasant soiled from his journey, suited for obscurity. The mantle of authority, at least for me, had shifted from my resplendent Father Phinehas to this tattered peasant beside me. Abba is wise and discerning and while no further words had passed, I wonder if he sensed that this event with his eldest son would be memorable. As memorable as the return of his son Caleb?

"Well, I shall leave you two to yourselves". Father nodded toward Labbaeus Thaddaeus and retreated into the villa. I caught a glimpse of the dark eyes of Simeon, the ever-curious servant, inside the doorway, eavesdropping as usual.

"You must be weary from your journey. Have you come from Jerusalem?"

"Yes, from Jerusalem. It has been a very hot journey."

"Let me offer you some refreshments and a place to rest for awhile." He nods. I lead him around the villa to the guest cottages, past the sparse huts for servants of guests. I wonder if Abba thought I would board him as a servant?

"After you have rested please tell me what is happening in Jerusalem, There is much I want to ask you."

"Yes sir" he drawls as we reach the elegant guest cottage. The cottage is of thick cut stone walls and a tiled roof, blocking the heat and keeping the air inside cool amongst the towering palm and acacia trees, with large rosemary shrubs around the perimeter of the cottage. The ever prescient Simeon has dispatched a servant to attend to Thaddaeus. I muse that Thaddaeus has never had this kind of service and really does not know what happens next. At his servants' direction he will bathe and eat pita, cheese and fruit; then nap for an hour or so. We will have time to talk before dinner. I wonder if Abba will approve inviting him to dine with the family. I summon Simeon and tell him to set a place for Thaddaeus. Simeon hesitates with a puzzled look, glancing back at the villa as if to get confirmation from Abba. "Just do it, Simeon."

"Of course, sir." I note the slight grin as he anticipates -with relish - a change in the evening routine with the possibility of sparks from the friction of family and custom. Simeon, although a slave, has a devilish independent streak and a chameleon-like ability to expose it when it suits him. It never suits him when in the presence of Abba, who trusts him too much.

While Thaddaeus rests I think back on the remarkable events in Jerusalem and the sparse news of what's going on now. It has been almost three months since I returned to Ephraim. Matthew has sent word twice to wait and to be in prayer for the safety of the apostles and new disciples in Jerusalem and for direction from Holy Spirit. The same message has gone to Joseph in Arimathea and Nicodemus in Hebron. I am in a strange and uncharted place, spiritually if not physically. The miracle of Holy Spirit coming in the upper room that morning stands as a solid rock for my beliefs and once again I relive that vivid day. The wind howled inside the room. Bolts of fire flickered and sought rest on our tunics without igniting. Men shouted in Aramaic who knew no Aramaic. It was as if we were transported inside of a towering thunderstorm cloud. When the calm came all were quiet. The eyes of those around me reflected my own astonished confusion. I had no idea what had happened. But something profound had invaded that pious and patient gathering. Then the man called Peter spoke. He began with the passage from the Prophet:

'AND IT SHALL BE IN THE LAST DAYS,' God says,
'THAT I WILL POUR FORTH OF MY SPIRIT ON ALL
MANKIND;

*AND YOUR SONS AND YOUR DAUGHTERS SHALL
PROPHESY,
AND YOUR YOUNG MEN SHALL SEE VISIONS,
AND YOUR OLD MEN SHALL DREAM DREAMS;
EVEN ON MY BONDSLAVES, BOTH MEN AND
WOMEN,
I WILL IN THOSE DAYS POUR FORTH OF MY SPIRIT
'AND I WILL GRANT WONDERS IN THE SKY ABOVE
AND SIGNS ON THE EARTH BELOW,
BLOOD, AND FIRE, AND VAPOR OF SMOKE.*

Then Peter ended with these words, which I remember as if they were not only revealed to my mind but sealed upon my heart:

"Therefore let all the house of Israel know for certain that God has made Him both Lord and Christ — this Jesus whom you crucified."

I "knew" then that Jesus is the Messiah, him crucified and raised from the dead. Yes, it is a way of knowing without fully understanding. Matthew says I am getting a better grasp of what faith means.

I reflect back to my encounter with Jesus on the road to Jerusalem, my only personal encounter with him. That meeting no longer seems tragic, but hopeful. His face, his bearing, his voice are firmly sealed upon my mind. The aimless, blind longing that had often haunted me from my youth has been replaced with a longing to be with the risen Christ, Jesus of Nazareth. What does it mean to 'be with' the risen Christ?

The longing, while aimed at being with Jesus, is still that which gnaws and hollows out my gut. I long to eat the bread of life. John told me about Jesus proclaiming that he was the bread of life and he who eats it will never hunger again. Where is this bread here and

now in Ephraim? I begin to drift off to the questions which always
dominate my thoughts. I realize, again, that I know nothing but the
longing. Nothing but a vague faith that Jesus is the Christ. I pray
that Thaddaeus will give me some direction.

Thaddaeus is a sturdy young man, older looking than his twenty-
five years. That is how he gave his age when I asked him earlier. At
this moment, emerging from the cottage dressed in our guests attire
he was better dressed, was cleaner, and smelled better than he had in
his life, I imagined. He is rather tall with a red-tanned complexion
that testifies to his life of outside labor. His black hair is cropped in
the Roman fashion, which is curious. His beard is full but reveals
an angular face with a prominent nose and wide mouth. His deep
set eyes hint at one who ponders much. There are two hours before
dinner. I am anxious to hear about developments in Jerusalem since
my departure, but there is a nagging detail to get out of the way:

"Thaddaeus, why did you come here to see me?"

"Well, let's see. The twelve…" Thaddaeus paused with his
pondering eyes moving away from mine. As the wait became
unsettling I called him back from wherever his thoughts had taken
him. "Thaddaeus?" "Oh, Ethan, sir. Excuse me but I still have a hard
time believing I am one of the twelve. I ponder on this too much,
but it still puzzles me that Jesus would call a simple rock mason to
be a disciple of Messiah."

"Well, perhaps Jesus thought he needed two rocks." Thaddaeus
laughs heartily at my attempt at humor.

"Ah, Peter, first my hardheaded mate, now my leader" Thaddaeus
muses. "I talked to him about not feeling worthy of being one of the
twelve." Another long pause.

"Thaddaeus, what did he say?"

"He said: 'Well, Jesus chose you, you did not choose him, so be
it!' Peter's like that."

"Thaddaeus, I believe this conversation started about why you were sent to seek me out."

"Yes sir, you are right."

I interrupt. "Thaddaeus, please drop the 'Sir'. I should address you as Sir, not the other way around. But I won't - let's make this a little easier on both of us." Sitting face to face with one of the honored twelve, I realize that my worldly status as a privileged and wealthy ruler will never be far from the surface of our relationship.

After yet another serious pause, pondering matters of class and status I suppose, Thaddaeus replies: "As you say, Ethan." Do I capture some sense of ironical skepticism in his well pondered response? We'll see.

Finally, Thaddaeus begins: "The twelve...Oh, did I tell you about replacing Judas - not me for I am also called Judas. " I think we are about to go off on another tangent. But of course I want to know.

"Pray tell me."

"Over a hundred or so folk had been meeting and praying in the upper room waiting as our Lord told us to. The last thing we did before Holy Spirit came was to choose Matthias to take the place of Judas Iscariot. He and Justus Barsabbas had been put forth and both were good men who had followed Jesus sometimes. They both had seen Jesus after the resurrection. God's lot fell to Matthias and he is now amongst the twelve."

I must have arrived just after this. I knew neither of these disciples.

"Peter had preached stoutly after Holy Spirit came down," Thaddaeus went on.

Now it was my time to ponder. The words of Peter that day still rang clear in my mind and soul. Words of the power of Holy Spirit to point us to Jesus for visions, dreams, and prophesies; and for the mystery of mysteries for us Israelites - eternal life. I am again surprised at the vividness of my memory and the strength of my conviction of what happened that day in that upper room.

Thaddaeus was talking on: "We began to pray about what we are supposed to do now. You were a part of this as you and Joseph and Nicodemus talked with Matthew. He told us about you three and what he had told you to do. This led us to begin to pray for each of us twelve about what we are to do. Of an evening the each of us talked about what our gifts might be." Thaddaeus lapsed into the distinct idioms of Galilean Aramaic often. "We know you have already spread the gospel in your household. Daniel your cousin and Caleb your brother came looking for baptism. That brother of yours seems a rambunctious type. Fiery little fellow." I thought to myself, 'To put it mildly.'

His eyes retreat from mine and his mind is off to that pondering place. He seems unaware of the length of his pauses and how discomfiting they could be to the listener. He's back.   "The other eleven thinks I am a story teller. I reckon I am. I can't read much but I remember things real good. I always thought of myself as a bystander – not a leader of the pack. Being a bystander let's me listen and see what's going on. But I'll tell you this: It was hard to figure what was going on with Jesus. And not just me. All of us twelve and the rest spent many an evening trying to figure out what Jesus meant by what he said and did that day. And don't think Jesus didn't notice us being confused and, well, even stubborn. He got downright frustrated with us sometimes and let us have it." Another pause. "He said some things so hard that a lot of folk shook their heads and left us. Some of the twelve talked about leaving. But Peter said 'Where would we go?' That about summed it up for me - there was no where else to go. That being true, the bigger truth is that I did not want anything else but to be with Jesus and the disciples. He taught me how to love truly." I mused that this Galilean peasant, while unsophisticated in the ways of the world, was thoughtfully intelligent.

"So, Thaddaeus, you were sent here to tell me stories – stories of what Jesus did?"

"I reckon so" he said flatly. But then added "And in the telling to see what the Lord wants us to do – us, you and me." His words and his now piercing eyes warn me not to take this young 'peasant' lightly.

It is dinner time. This is going to be interesting.

+ + +

Dinner was not so interesting after all. I had prepared my mind for a drama where the clash of sub-cultures, Israelite ruling class versus Israelite peasantry, came face to face over the ritual of dinner. There was no drama, except for the drama of why there was no drama. Why? The quiet confidence of Thaddaeus bar Alphaeus the peasant and the respectful humility of Phinehas bar Ezer the ruler portray two men who know who they are - despite their sub-Israelite class differences. Beyond self assurance, both are inclined to be gracious and respectful towards others. In such a meeting of minds and souls distinctions of status, rank, and wealth become facile. There will be no trouble here, even though all remains the same and no one has altered their values. Such is the nature of humility and grace: the great levelers of men.

Had my Mother Livia been here there may have been a more arresting mood at table. She was still visiting her family in Tyre. Tyre is on the Great Sea far to the north in Phoenicia below the river Litani that flows out of the high mountains of Lebanon.

Her family's ancestry went back to Asher, the seventh son of Jacob. Far removed from the centers of Judaism in Judah, Tyre is the least religious of all of Palestine. Mother's family was certainly very different from the ruling families of our part of Palestine. Mother fit naturally into the privileged court culture. Her beauty and strong will made an immediate impression on those in her presence. But she was not an overly proud woman. She simply accepted her privileged state and had no inclination to question the customs of her time. She was kind to her servants and to her equals. This inclination to kindness, and even a nuanced humility, was the trait she shared most with my Father. Abba and Mama were very good parents indeed.

The House of Asher is perhaps the wealthiest of all the Israelites. They not only possess the wealth of inherited land but of their industry in ship building. The sea is strange and foreboding in Israelite history. We are a people of the hills and the deserts. Not so with Asher's descendants. They took to the sea in generations not remembered and their family lore is all about the Sea. In recent generations they moved from fishing to ship building, rivaling their gentile Phoenician neighbors. My great grandfather saw the benefits of the Roman conquest and ignored the burdens. The growth of Roman law throughout the world had made sea transport much safer. My grandfather told of his father saying "The sea is always the same. The land has drought, plagues, and fickle seasons to steal away the crops. The hills are hard on the legs. The desert is a foolish place to be. The sea is always the same. Plow the sea."

And he did and the world now knew of the fine ships of the Tyrean Hebrews.

+ + +

The next morning dawned with clouds promising relief from the heat of the past several days. I see Thaddaeus walking about the garden in the courtyard admiring the colorful flowers. I suppose it reminds him of the Galilean countryside with its forests and fertile lands nourished by the Sea of Chinnereth, now called the Sea of Galilee by the natives. Despite the forests and fertile lands, Galilee historically has been one of the poorest regions of Palestine. Herod Antipas was the latest of the Israelite puppet kings that ruled Galilee with a peculiar cruelty and oppressive taxes. This led to discouragement and lack of industry among the Israelites. The economy became one of subsistence farming and the wages of those who labored at the large Roman army facilities. Sephorris is the largest town in Galilee but is practically all Roman and other gentiles employed by the army. The Israelites of Galilee are regarded as ignorant peasant stock. The old ruling class, such as us here in Ephraim, has withered away. There are no families in Galilee that approach the wealth and authority of the House of Phinehas bar Ezer.

Thaddaeus is in deep thought as I approach him. He does not turn to me until I am abreast and walking slowly with him. He casts a friendly smile as I greet him good morning. "And a good morning to you, Ethan." The class tension of yesterday has receded as if he has made a thoughtful decision to accept the status of equality that I sincerely offered.

"Thaddaeus, I hope you understand how difficult it is for me to be here wondering what is going on in Jerusalem. I am used to being in the middle of things. Actually I am used to running things, not being a bystander as you describe yourself. It has been weeks since I returned as Matthew directed. I have heard from Joseph in Arimathea and Nicodemus in Hebron and they are the same. This requires real discipline to stay and wait." After the pause that I am getting used to, Thaddaeus replies that he knows no more than he has told me and that we must be content to wait until Holy Spirit gives us direction. He continues, "Lord Jesus taught us go to the Scriptures for guidance in all of life. I am also restless like you. I have thought of the words of the prophet Hosea for these times:

> *Sow with a view to righteousness,*
> *Reap in accordance with kindness;*
> *Break up your fallow ground,*
> *For it is time to seek the LORD*
> *Until He comes to rain righteousness on you.*

"Perhaps I see how this helps us, but tell me what it means to you, Thaddaeus."

"Jesus always sowed seeds of righteousness among the people he was with. He was always kind to those who heard his teachings. We will also live in this way as we follow his commandments. But now is also a time of waiting. While we wait we are to survey the land of our inheritance – our souls. Where is the fallow ground of your soul, Ethan? Find it and break it up so that it will be ready for planting when Holy Spirit brings the rain of righteousness. Then our souls will grow, expand. Then we will know the path before us."

I am stunned by the eloquence and depth of Thaddaeus' explication of the words of Hosea! In a moment he has given me a keen insight into my own soul, into my very being. His farming metaphor is ideally suited to me, for farming is a major part of my family's enterprise. Where indeed is the fallow ground of my soul. Thaddaeus has given me an assignment, and I believe he knows it even though I have not spoken.

"Thaddaeus, I came this morning to hear some of the stories of Jesus, but you have sent me another way for now. I need to think, and pray, about my soul, about my fallow ground." He buried the receding class distinction by putting his strong stonemason's arm around my shoulder with a tug of encouragement. Then he walked off without another word. I watched as he strode through the gate and onto the path to the highest of the hills around us as if on a mission. I realize that I am now watching my friend and my spiritual mentor. I go to my favorite quiet place beyond the south wall; a slight valley where a small creek runs when the rains are plentiful.

Break up your fallow ground. The words of Hosea haunt me. At first, knowing that I had fallow ground seemed neglectful, even sinful. But then, any good farm has fallow ground left unplanted for a time to restore its fertility. Or ground never planted but awaiting future use. The latter is where the metaphor fits me. I thought that my experience with Jesus on the road leading me to that remarkable morning in the upper room had uprooted my soul. There was no fallow ground left. The brief time with the disciples - especially the time with Matthew confirmed this- I thought.

I know I am a different man, but even in the short time since those days, my old self is reasserting itself. My morning prayers and evening reading of the Torah have become less intense and shorter. I find the awaiting business chores winding their way into my devotions. Is what was growing becoming gradually fallow? Oh, I hope not! For I thirst for the love of Jesus and the hope that in his love I will be made whole – banishing the gnawing longing for the unknown that has always followed me.

My meditation moves to prayer: 'Dear God, Dear Jesus, fill the hollowness of my soul with your love and grace, that I will be made anew.' I recall Nicodemus telling of his encounter with Jesus. Jesus said we must be born again; born of the spirit. Am I born again? Surely the Spirit was upon me in the upper room. I am a different man. Surely the fallow ground of my soul was plowed up. For what?

I fall quiet to listen for God's guidance. I strive to shut down my active mind and move to a contemplative place where I can savor the presence of God. After a time I realize it is time to move on. I have a sense of peace and assurance that God will show me the way, even if it is not now. I stand ready to plant the fallow ground when he comes to rain his righteous way on me.

PART THREE

Thaddaeus has now been here three days and I realize I have had little time to hear him tell of his time with Jesus. We agreed to set aside some time each day we are here for his 'story telling', as he calls it. Naamah, one of the refectory servants, has set up two comfortable chairs of soft woven laurel arranged under the large chestnut tree just outside the wall and not far from the dreadful site of my raging at the return of Caleb. Pitchers of minted tea and pomegranate juice, cool from the springhouse, rest on a matching small table. Naamah is a delightful servant respected by servants and family alike for her pleasant, gracious personality. She is also very beautiful. Mother named her Naamah for these qualities soon after she arrived as a young slave girl of about twelve years. No one can remember her name upon arriving ten years ago. Playfully, she will not divulge her previously given name, saying that she only began to live when she was received into the household of Phinehas bar Ezer. Was she 'born again'?

"Thaddaeus, please tell me one of your stories about Jesus."

As usual, Thaddaeus does not get directly to the task. "Ethan, let me tell you that I have a strange way to tell of my times with Jesus. At least, that is what many say of my story telling. The way I am able to remember a lot of the happenings is because I was there. I do not mean just that I witnessed what Jesus did and said, but that I was in the, the ...story."

"What do you mean 'in the story'"?

"Well, at night we all would often share our thoughts about the happenings of the day. Jesus mostly listened and did not offer his comments very much at these gatherings. Often he went away to pray. It was amazing to me how differently the disciples, not just the twelve but others who were always with Jesus, saw Jesus' doings and sayings. While everybody agreed on what happened, each took him a little different. Peter usually wanted a clear reason for what Jesus said. John seemed more interested in Jesus' countenance and the way people saw love in him. Thomas would usually find something to question or object to - Matthew called him the devil's advocate. It was a friendly joke, I think. Judas Iscariot was impatient, sometimes angry because we were not zealous about rebelling against the Romans. I think he was a member of the Zealots but he never admitted it."

"I mostly listened. I am a good listener," Thaddaeus reminds me again.

After what is a long pause for me but a short one for him, he continues: "Sometimes the happenings of the day caused me to get away by myself to think more about what had happened and what Jesus said. People have always said that I have a lot of imagination. I think everyone has imagination but many do not use it. I really like to imagine things. As a boy they were the usual pretend things: being a sailor and going across the Big Sea; being a brave warrior and attacking the, the…" He leaves the sentence unfinished as he glances at our opulent surroundings that would not be possible without some deference to the Romans.

He recovers quickly: "But now I like to put myself into the story, to be one of the actors like in the Greek plays. Ethan, have you ever seen a Greek drama?" I think, 'am I ever going to hear a Jesus story?'

"Yes, I have attended several. I can tell you about them another time." I realize that I have presumed this peasant had not seen a Greek play. I was right.

"I have only heard of them, but I would really like to see one. I hear they use the imagination a lot." I resist the urge to call Thaddaeus back to the task at hand. But he comes back unassisted:

"Let me tell you a Jesus story. Mind now that the doings and sayings of Jesus are true and are not from my imagination. My imagination puts me in the story and burns the story into my mind and seals it in my heart so I don't forget."

"One day not long before he chose the twelve, I was with the followers near Capernaum, on the Sabbath. We went into the Synagogue to worship and there was a man with a badly withered hand. Jesus looked toward the congregation and summoned the man to come up. Jesus turned to those gathered and said: 'Is it lawful to do good or to do harm on the Sabbath, to save a life or to kill?' The congregation was silent – including all his followers, for this is a hard question. Jesus turned to the man and said: 'Stretch out you hand.' He did and his hand was healed - completely healed. There were gasps and praises, but immediately we saw some Pharisees leave. As we left we saw the Pharisees gathered together and some cast troubled glances toward us. We later found out that they were with some from Herod's court and were talking about punishing Jesus, even killing him."

Thaddaeus continues: "I was really moved, even upset at Jesus' actions. The struggle between doing a good thing and observing Sabbath laws was there for all to see. And Jesus did not hesitate in his choice. Jesus was angry but at the same time calm, without doubt about what was right. I was anxious, nervous, and filled up with doubt. What does this mean?"

"Later I was able to get away by myself and try to understand better by reliving that drama in the Synagogue. So I began my story:"

Thaddaeus' Story

"I am a Pharisee. I am one of the group who has just witnessed Jesus from Nazareth illegally heal a man on the Sabbath. I am an accepted Holy man of my community, an honorable and respected synagogue leader. This man, Jesus, has been attacking my group's claim as the spiritual leaders of our people. Yet we are the ones who have been true and faithful to our long traditions of faith. We are the true followers of Yahweh. It is we who have labored long and hard to faithfully perfect the Law of Moses. It is we who have spoken the Laws of Moses clearly so that the people can understand and obey. God will surely honor our efforts to strictly adhere to the letter of the Law which Yahweh gave to our Fathers, even the great Moses.

Our group gathers outside to meet with the agents of Herod assigned to investigate the trouble caused by Jesus and his followers. My anger is growing inside me as I think about the abomination that just happened in the synagogue. Aaron, the true Rabbi here, reminds us of our faith to the Law of God and our duty to expose pretenders and heretics. The Herodians are exclaiming about the growing potential for civic unrest that will surely bring down the wrath of the Romans to the harm of us all. My thoughts are squarely on this man Jesus, an uneducated peasant carpenter from Nazareth (indeed, can anything good come from Nazareth?), who flaunts his pretentious claim to be a Rabbi. This Jesus who mocks the laws of the Sabbath! This Jesus has violated the Law by healing the withered hand right here in the synagogue, the very house of the Lord! Rabbi Aaron reminds us that Jesus not only healed the man but he had the audacity to become angry at us for trying to protect the Law! I wonder what provoked his anger? Was it our refusal to answer his simplistic question about doing good on the Sabbath? How could one of his lowly state understand the complexity of the Law which in this case surpasses his desire to do random acts of kindness.

The discussion has turned heated and some are arguing that his violations are serious enough for legal action. Some suggest capital punishment. But as this discussion continues, I notice the peasant whose hand was healed leaving the synagogue with his friends and family. They are overjoyed and amazed that the once disfigured hand is restored. He jabs his arm into the air repeatedly and opens and clinches his healed hand and shouts hosannas to the departing crowd. He is truly joyful and is obviously untroubled by the violation of the Law. Will he ever repent? Will he realize that God can bring upon him far greater affliction than a withered hand for his disobedience? Does he not consider the wrath of God that has been visited upon our people in the past for our disobedience of the Law? Does he not consider the curse of God we are under now - the oppression of the Romans that make these Herodian agents mere puppets of Pontius Pilate? Does he think that life is as simple as just being healed? Woe to you, Jesus and your victims!

But my heart is restless within me. I cannot put the joy of the healing out of my mind. I am disturbed that my training and upbringing to strive to be obedient to the law is challenged by this Galilean and his healing. I cannot escape the haunting question that I know is on the mind of many of us: if he is not of God, how can he do these things? Our leaders say he practices sorcery by the power of Satan. Perhaps. I have remained silent during the discussions, preoccupied by my own thoughts and doubts. I feel a strong desire to know more about Jesus of Nazareth. As our group leaves, I slip away to question Jesus. I find him in a small olive grove by the well, with two of his followers. They are silently resting. Jesus does not yet see me. After a drink of water, he sits silently in his own thoughts or perhaps waiting for someone. I decide to take this opportunity and address him without introduction. "How can you transgress the law of the Sabbath, even for a good deed?" The two get up as to leave but Jesus beckons them to stay. No one but me has spoken a word. I am somewhat chagrined by my confronting attitude, but wonder why I am concerned about being polite to this pretender. He lifts his gaze to me slowly and calmly, not responding for what seems like a long while. "Our Father, Yahweh, Abba, loves beyond the law", he answers softly, matter of factly. His utterance of the Father as Abba startles me. No one in their right mind would address Yahweh the way a child would address their earthly father. But I know from his countenance that this man is not out of his mind. In fact, I sense an authentic authority in his voice. Pausing as if to give me time to size him up, he then continues. "You are a leader among the Pharisees, and you are right to love the law." Again he pauses as if to allow me to silently acknowledge that he is right on both counts. Our eyes are now met, and I wonder where he is going with this, feeling no need to respond.

"You have lost your first love, the love of your Father, Abba, for the love of the pursuits of your own mind." Now he seems to wait for a response. But I am silent in the realization that duty, not love, is my watchword. The shame of being outwitted by a Galilean peasant flits through my mind but recedes as I see the tenderness in his eyes..

"What is your name", he asks? "Joseph, Joseph Barsabbas", I reply.

"Joseph, my Father's name", Jesus replies. "Ah, but 'Joseph Barsabbas', son of the Sabbath". He smiles, "No wonder you are devoted to the laws of the Sabbath." His tone is ironic, but kind. I wonder about why I seem content to let him speak and to not respond. The animosity I carried seems to have dissipated.

"Joseph Barsabbas", he says compassionately, "you know in your heart that love is the true foundation of the law, that the Sabbath is meaningless without the love and grace of our heavenly Father. Joseph Barsabbas, you know in your heart that love is greater than your laws." He said my name as one with authority over me. I am perplexed.

"Surely you are not the Messiah as some say?", I hear myself asking.
He smiles again, reassuringly, but does not answer. Rather he rises and
turns to leave. Then he turns back to me.
   "Come, follow me."
   I follow him.

"Well, that's the story. I will tell this and other stories about Jesus as long as I live. I cannot forget any of it."

Again, I am stunned at this peasant's intelligent articulation of a simple story come alive. Surely, Holy Spirit dwells deeply in this young man.

+ + +

The next morning I ask Thaddaeus to walk with me through the wooded area beyond the meadow. I had thought about his story telling gift and how we could share these gospel stories. As we enter the woods the little warmth in the air dissipates quickly as we gain some altitude. The day is overcast and unseasonably cool – good for a hike. We make small talk, admiring the ferns along the trail, the large acacia and sycamore trees that grew well here on the heights of Ephraim, catching the moist winds from the Great Sea 40 miles to the west.

"Thaddaeus, I believe we should go on a journey to share your times with Jesus for those who have not heard the gospel."

"Where would we go?"

"I have given that some thought. I really want to go to Jerusalem just to find out what is happening there. We know from our business contacts, confirmed by my Uncle Levi, that the disciples are having to keep out of sight because of Caiaphas' desire to snuff out the Way. There seems to be little we could do in Jerusalem. Matthew sees Nicodemus in Hebron, Joseph in Arimathea, and us here in Ephraim as ideally placed for spreading the gospel. I think we should go north in Ephraim, over to Samaria and back home. Or to Jerusalem if there is news to bring us there."

After the inevitable pause, Thaddaeus responds, "I believe that is a good plan. Do you believe the Lord is leading you to this journey?"

"Yes, I do."

"Me too. When do we leave?"

I answer, "In a few days. I have contacts in various villages and I can arrange ...

"Ethan" he says firmly, "this is not the way of the Lord. Let us just go with enough for the day and go to the people. The Lord will provide for us, he will show us the way to go each day."

I realize that I have never done a thing in my life that did not have some element of a plan. How efficient can this be? A voice in my head says: "As efficient as I choose." Can a voice in my head be sarcastic; mocking the word 'efficient'? I am on unchartered ground. Thaddaeus' way is the peasant's way. So, do I become a peasant for awhile? Am I capable of that? Will I simply be an actor on the stage of a Greek drama? Comedy or tragedy? Can I stop speculating and just do it? Leave all your riches behind, and come follow me, to paraphrase those chilling words on my encounter with Jesus. I see possibilities that I did not see before.

"As you say Thaddaeus, we'll do it the Jesus Way!"

His eyes glisten with excitement at being on the road again to share his love of Jesus, the Messiah.

"I do have one plan I would like to keep. The Torah discussion group meets tomorrow at Shiloh. You can tell a Jesus story there. They will listen to you."

"Good, Ethan. We should each spend this day in prayer for our journey. We leave tomorrow." Pray all day? Is that possible? I'll see.

+ + +

First, I request permission of Abba to take on this journey of a month or so. This is rather a formality because Abba knows I would not absent myself if there were pressing matters that required my attention. Daniel has returned weekly for a few days to catch up on work since their leaving about five weeks ago. Caleb has been baptized and is now safe with the apostles. Daniel reports that Caleb has become close to John and James, the 'sons of thunder' as Jesus called them. That figures. Daniel and Caleb are due to return in a few days. They will stay and resume their duties making it convenient for me to take the mission journey with Thaddaeus. We have a deep pool of stewards who will be delegated my usual tasks, under the direction of Caleb and Daniel.

Abba is interested in my motives for the journey.

"My Son, you are very serious about this Jesus and his Way, aren't you?" I nod, inviting him to go on. "You know I do not understand how this rabbi is different than those who have gone before – and have faded away. Yes, I am surprised that one of your intelligence and learning is attracted to this man, or perhaps even a prophet." We have had little time to really talk of my 'conversion' but it is apparent that he has thought on it.

"I know you do not understand. I know your are surprised. Father, a confession: I do not understand myself, and I too am surprised. But this I know: My mind – and my heart – will not let go of this man, and he will not let go of me. I am a captive of Jesus of Nazareth, the Messiah."

"A captive? Or a slave?" Phinehas bar Ezer is wrestling with a concept that has no category in his worldview as a wealthy ruler. "Can a slave to another become head of this household with my passing, the household of Ethan Asher bar Phinehas? I know you have considered this. What is your plan?"

"I have no plan. I cannot answer your questions. Jesus promised to lead us rightly if we become his followers. I believe Thaddaeus was sent here to guide me. I will follow him for this journey. But this I will promise you: I will not leave you and this household as Caleb did. I will not request my inheritance before my time. One of the disciples, Matthew, believes I can be a witness for Jesus the Messiah and continue my leadership of your household. I will do nothing more than complete this journey without conferring with you first, God willing."

Phinehas bar Ezer's fixed dark eyes penetrate me as he decides if I am confused or mad. I doubt that he considers other possibilities. "Have a safe journey" he says flatly. He turns abruptly and leaves the room.

+ + +

The long days of summer bring dawn at the first hour. I slept fitfully, tossing about with the thoughts of my talk with Abba. My attempt at prolonged prayer yesterday was also fitful for the same reason. The temporal concerns of the day seem to eat up the eternal blessings of God's grace. In this new day I turn to God readily. My prayers are long and rambling and I am surprised when I hear the bell ringing for breakfast at half past the second hour.

I greet Thaddaeus who is already here. Naamah is serving and informs me that Abba will not be joining us this morning. I am not surprised. In the month or so since Caleb and Daniel left to seek baptism in Jerusalem, Daniel has returned twice to catch up on work and give an account of the happenings in Jerusalem. He is due back about now to oversee the wine inventory and will hopefully have news of Caleb and the other disciples.

So we breakfast alone. The hot Ethiopian coffee and wheat rolls with sweet crushed buckberries are delicious and energizing.

We are both excited about the beginning of the journey; perhaps in different ways. Thaddaeus' excitement is pure joy, unfettered by worldly concerns. A man who wills one thing is someone to behold. I am the novice now. The role reversal alone promises excitement for me. We plan to leave after Daniel returns and we both pray that he is not delayed. We will then begin our five mile walk to Shiloh. I reckon it will take two plus hours – twice the time of a leisurely ride on Nekoda. Have I ever walked to Shiloh? No, why should I have?

+ + +

I recognize the rider on the horse, approaching at a steady gallop. He is a servant from my Grandfather's home in Tyre. There will be news from Mother. News indeed! Mother arrives tomorrow. She has received word of the happenings surrounding Caleb and me. She is concerned about Caleb and has waited long enough for word that he is safe. Mother will be angry – no, livid, I think. But a controlled lividness. There will be a family council. I suspect that the verdict will be that this mess is all my fault. And, of course, it is. Or, is it Jesus' 'fault'?

We all gather to greet Mother as her carriage and small entourage appears on the long white approach road that has recently witnessed two other dramatic arrivals. Abba is overjoyed and embraces Mother much like he must have hugged Caleb, who arrived in a much different state.

"Mama, I have missed you." There is a slight but noticeable stiffness as I kiss her lightly on each cheek. The embrace is incomplete. I notice the added wrinkles around her large dark eyes. I notice a little sagging of the skin of her neck. She is still remarkably beautiful at sixty years – or is it sixty-one? Her darting eyes cancel the smile on her lips as we separate. Is she livid? That Caleb is not home only increases the tension.

Mother Livia should be weary from her long journey from Tyre. Following our usual route she would have left Tyre in one of her family's fine ships and sailed down the coast to the bay at Ptolemais where they would stay a day or two with family. I remember the impressive view south across the bay to the river Kishon as it passed Mt. Carmel nearby. Another day's sail to Caesarea where they would be guests of the Roman Legatus who commanded both the Army Legion and the Roman Navy fleet stationed there. The Legatus is influential in Navy procurement and responsible for sales of Tyrean ships to the Roman Navy. Departing from Caesarea, another days sailing, in good weather, would land her in Joppa and complete the sea leg of her trip home. From Joppa the entourage would follow the road to Arimathea, the home of my good friend Joseph. Mother would surely have over-nighted there. What would she learn from Joseph's widowed mother about Joseph's conversion to the Way of Jesus? Another day's journey would bring her home to Ephraim. The trip details were confirmed by Allon, the leader of Mother's household servants. Allon was fifteen years my senior, and was as much a hero to me as a boy as a servant could be. He was very strong and an outstanding athlete. He was the boxing champion of Ephraim in his younger days. We all believed that Mama was safe in her travels with Allon as her protector.

The family council will be held at the third hour tomorrow. I had informed Thaddaeus that our mission trip would be delayed on the news of Mother's return. Thaddaeus fully grasped the tension of the moment. Without prompting, he advised Naama that he would not be at dinner or breakfast and to please not set a place for him. Naama understood.

Dinner was tense. Mother told of happenings in her family – a marriage, a death, and greetings especially from Seth, my cousin and Mother's nephew. Seth and I were often called 'twins' because we were born on the same day, though miles apart, and bore a remarkable resemblance to one another. In our childhood years we often spent summers together. Mother and her sister Peninnah, Seth's mother, were also similar in looks and personality.

She recited the events of her unremarkable trip home. This was all done in the detached manner of a hired messenger. Abba said very little, nodding and mumbling occasionally; interrupting Mama twice to express again his sincere delight in having his beloved Livia home. Once he turned to me and said: "Is it not good to have Mama back again"? I had never heard Abba call her Mama.

After dinner I go in search of Thaddaeus. I see him sitting in the side garden which has a clear view of the late evening sunset. A clear day, the setting sun bristles and expands against the evening blue sky as it plunges toward the unseen Great Sea. I pause before approaching him to reflect alone on the sunset view, as Thaddaeus is doing.

The irony of the Israelite vision of the sea as a menace is striking when one considers its benefits, even at a distance of two or three days. The moist and cooling sea breezes make life here in Ephraim pleasant; to say nothing of the benefits for the crops – especially the fine wine grapes that flourish here. Yet many of the Israelites hereabouts have never seen the Great Sea. I also recognize the irony that I have lapsed into a peaceful pastoral frame of mind. I know a furious storm of Tyrean proportions awaits me on the morrow, a storm called Livia.

"Thaddaeus, have I disturbed you?"

"No, no" as he rises and turns away from the sun. "The sun sets on hills at my house in Galilee. It is not quite so brilliant."

"I see by your absence from dinner that you are fully aware of the, er, tension with my Mother's return. Naama told me of your request. Although it is uncomfortable for me to say so, I thank you for your deference."

With only a slight nod to accept my thanks, Thaddaeus gets to the point: "Are you certain that your Mother Livia shall be so harsh as you imagine."

"Yes, I am certain. There is here a clash of deep tradition, family honor, and, not to be taken lightly, business. My Father, and especially Mother, are very conservative in their views about our Israelite inheritance of settled social and religious ways. Why shouldn't they be so? They, and I, have done very well by those ways."

"Ethan, I do not mean to judge you or your parents, but perhaps I can offer some ideas that will help you keep on honoring your Father and Mother."

" I have never intended to dishonor them. That is not the issue!" I am offended by his suggestion of dishonor.

"Ethan," he says firmly, "in their eyes this is exactly about honor. Did you hear from the apostles about some of Jesus' hard sayings?"

"What do you have in mind?"

"Jesus once said that he came with a sword, causing discord and not shalom. I remember exactly what he said, because it is a very hard saying to understand. I am surprised Matthew did not tell you because he has given it much thought. Jesus said: 'He who loves father or mother more than Me is not worthy of Me; and he who loves son or daughter more than Me is not worthy of Me. And he who does not take his cross and follow after Me is not worthy of Me. He who has found his life will lose it, and he who has lost his life for My sake will find it.'

My despondence turns instantly to anger.

"Thaddaeus! The Jesus I met was kind and the very essence of shalom! He could not have said such a thing! Holy Spirit that day in the upper room united people from different tribes and tongues! There was no sword that divided! This is absurd!"

My outburst seemed to have no effect on Thaddaeus. He was as calm as a Greek Stoic buying onions in the marketplace. He waited patiently to see if I was done with my rant.

"I'm sorry for my outburst, Thaddaeus. But I need an explanation for this hard saying."

"Jesus said this while telling the twelve about the hardships to come for us and the other disciples. Embracing the gospel of Jesus will indeed bring peace to our hearts. But in this time of change from the old ways to the new way of Jesus there will be trouble. Most will want to hang on to the old ways, especially those who have profited by those old ways." Thaddaeus looks to see if I realize that he is talking of my family. Of course I do. He continues, "Those will demand that the old ways prevail. They will insist that their children continue the old ways."

I interrupt, "And my loyalty must be to Jesus rather than my family?"

"If it comes to that" Thaddaeus says gravely.

"This is a hard saying, my friend." I pause for a long reflection.

"Does it have to come to that, Thaddaeus? I don't mean just for me, for my family. I mean for the Israelites as a whole? Must the sword divide the Israelites in half?"

Thaddaeus replies forlornly, "It already has, Ethan."

"Thaddaeus, I am very troubled. I cannot grasp why Jesus brought the sword. It contradicts everything I have believed about the gospel: Faith, hope, love. Forgiveness. Turning the other cheek. Living in the shalom of the Kingdom of God. These cannot stand with a sword wielding Jesus!"

After a moment of awkward silence, Thaddaeus presses on: "Perhaps there is another way to see this. Often Jesus would further explain his teachings of the day as we had our supper. This one he did not – and I suspect that no one wanted to hear more of this hard teaching. I mentioned that Matthew had wrestled with this teaching. He and I talked and prayed over this. Consider what has happened during the last days that Jesus was with us:"

- "Herod wielded the sword killing John the baptizer who announced the coming of Messiah."
- "The Chief Priests and the Sanhedrin wielded the sword when they falsely condemned Jesus."
- "The Romans wielded the sword as they crucified him and plunged the sword into his side."

Thaddaeus continues, "why did the Israelite rulers and the Romans do these things? Pride, greed, selfishness and most of all – fear. These are the things that stand with the sword. "What did Jesus do? He never resisted. Surely he could have called down ten thousand angels with mighty swords. He faced the cross with faith, he gave hope to the thief beside him at Golgotha. As he suffered he looked out with love, not only for his disciples and his Mother, but also with love for his persecutors. For he asked his Father to forgive them. And he did all this to die for our sins that we may come and dwell in the shalom of his Kingdom – now and forever. Do all the promises of the gospel stand when seen from this view, Ethan?

"Yes, they do. Jesus was not saying that he would wield the sword but that his new way would bring out the sword of his enemies. And that the divisions of the radical new way would not stop at the authorities but would cause divisions even in families. And yes, these things are already coming to pass. His message is a prophesy. "

"Ethan, this is what I came to believe. Perhaps there are other interpretations. I pray that I am honoring the Lord and not doing harm."

"Certainly no harm done here. I continue to be amazed at the depth of your insights into the gospel..." Thaddaeus completes my sentence, "from a Galilean peasant," with a grin that turns to mutual laughter. We have become good friends.

+ + +

The family council which was about to commence, was, of course, not a council. Councils were about business; and social and political happenings that affected the business. These would be attended by the extended family who were active managers of the various operations. This 'council' was to be one of reprimand. It would be more like the chastening when I was a budding teen chasing the maid - or was she chasing me? There would be no Rabbi this time to mediate my Mother's anger. 'Stop Ethan!' says the voice in my head. 'There will be a Rabbi present - Rabbi Jesus.' I pray, "O Lord, O Rabbi Jesus come to my assistance; O Lord, O Rabbi Jesus make haste to help me."

Mother and Father are already seated at the dining table. There are fruits and cakes and a large pot of steaming, aromatic Ethiopian coffee —evidence that none of us had broken the fast this morning. I stifled my strong desire for a cup of coffee since neither Mother nor Father are partaking.

"Good morning Mother, Father." Their hesitance in greeting me first portrays the tension and sadness that holds them. It also reinforces the great importance of what is before us. I can only imagine what hypothetical family tragedy they have projected. I too am dreading the demands and challenges I will face. I love my parents and deliberately hurting them is beyond my understanding. But Jesus' saying about the great divisions his gospel will cause loom large in my mind.

As I sit my Father rises. I have taken a seat opposite them to better sense their convictions and emotions. Abba begins:

"Ethan my dear son, your activities of the recent past have, as you know, been of great concern to me. And now to your Mother.

Firstly, I must confess to my own shortcomings in this matter. I should have intervened sooner and with more authority. It was much the same when I permitted Caleb to leave with his inheritance before his time. I hope my deference to your will, and Caleb's, is more from my love and respect for you than from my own weakness of character."

Phinehas bar Ezer, not Abba, was now holding court. He had assumed his role as the patriarch of this wealthy and ruling family. His regal bearing was somewhat of an act, for his honest humility and tender heart had always caused him some uneasiness as the ruling elder. Those who only saw him in one of his official capacities were not aware of this, for his executive bearing was genuine even in his hidden discomfort. I knew that this was a formal introductory phase. Soon he would pass the gavel to Mother for the hard stuff of this council of discipline. And he did.

"Ethan, your Mother is , of course, deeply troubled by this, umm, by your actions. I am sure you are well aware of this. We are especially concerned for Caleb. You encouraged him to go to Jerusalem to seek these Zealots." Neither of his statements were true, but there was no need to offer a correction. "Livia, perhaps you can talk to Ethan now." Mother had not as yet spoken. During Father's introduction she kept her eyes on me, looking for tell tale signs of my attitude. I thought I had been rather passive, because Father had said nothing provocative.

"Ethan dear, if you expected me to be very angry with you, I understand. I know that I can be stern when crossed, and firm in my convictions. I'm not angry, but I am beyond confused. You are a mature, intelligent young man. It is not always the case that the eldest son is prepared to assume the responsibilities of one in your Father's place. But no one, including me as the sternest critic in this household, has ever doubted your qualifications, your integrity, your character. To hear that you have turned to some far fetched cult for a 'new way' is completely out of character for you."

She said 'new way' sardonically, which I find curious. Has the 'way' and the 'new way' reached even unto Tyre? I assumed that she had never heard of Jesus the Nazarene, much less the nascent saying of the 'way' to identify his followers. The pause was my queue to respond.

"Father and Mother, Abba and mama, first let me say that I love you very much and it troubles me greatly that I am troubling you. I promised you, Abba, that I would not abandon my privileged position as eldest son and heir to the family estate. I pray earnestly that I will keep that promise. I intend to. But you also must know that I have been changed by my encounter with the rabbi Jesus bar Joseph, the Nazarene. I only met him briefly, but he impressed me mightily. I spent time with his disciples in Jerusalem, those on the 'way'." As I too put emphasis on 'way', Mother raised an eyebrow, confirming her acquaintance with its significance. I had forgotten that she had come through Arimathea and had undoubtedly shared her concerns with Joseph's mother. There was no point in satisfying my curiosity at this point.

"How did you come to involve Caleb in this?" Mother says, her judgment on me a settled matter.

" I shared with Caleb what I experienced in Jerusalem following Jesus' crucifixion. Daniel had already become a believer and had shared this with Caleb. He was anxious to go to Jerusalem and learn more about Jesus and his 'way'.

"Caleb is venturesome," says Abba without a hint of irony.

I go on, "I am very concerned, as you are, about Caleb's safety. There is talk of persecution of some of the apostles, although I have heard nothing of serious punishment. I pray that Daniel returns soon with news of Caleb's well being."

Mother says, "Ethan, we have so much to ask you about this sudden religious devotion and what you are thinking, and how this will affect all of our lives. But now is not the time for this. I am too anxious about news of Caleb to go on. Perhaps by tomorrow we will have good news and can go on. This matter must be settled soon." Mama is visibly tired, both from the trip home and this 'matter'.

"Yes dear. You must get some rest." Abba is visibly relieved to retreat from this conflict. So am I, even if it was milder than I had imagined.

+ + +

My first thought is to find Thaddaeus. I need to reflect and meditate on the meeting with my parents, but the situation with Thaddaeus is up in the air. Our journey north was left on hold and now the inconclusive meeting about the future (mine and the estate) makes it clear that this is not the time for a sabbatical. As I cross the courtyard Thaddaeus enters a back gate, probably from a hike in the hills.

Thaddaeus calls out: "Ethan, how did it go?" His quizzical look tells me he has been trying to imagine what took place.

"They were easy on me. Nothing was really resolved. That doesn't surprise me since I don't know exactly what, if anything, needs to be resolved. Mother's anger was not what I supposed, although it is clear that she believes I have come under a spell. And that I am responsible for bringing Caleb into 'this matter' as Abba called it. I need to reflect on this and see what the next steps should be."

"I did not think there would be a resolution now, and perhaps for some time to come." I can tell that Thaddaeus has come to a decision about what he should do now. My 'class' outlook had me assume he would wait for me to take the lead. He reveals his plan: " You and your family and household have been very kind and generous with me. We have had time to become good friends. It is now time to get on with the Lord's work. Our journey north will become a solitary one. I still feel called to go north and teach the good news of Jesus. I would like to stay until Caleb and Daniel return. I too am anxious about my brother James and the other apostles."

"Yes of course." My impulse is to encourage him to stay longer, but this is a pretense at manners. Thaddaeus is right, of course. "I understand. I cannot leave until I have somehow put Mother and Father at some ease. How, I do not know."

Thaddaeus' eyes are fixed on mine with sincere compassion and he encourages me without words. Finally he says, "You must attend to your family now. The Lord will be patient with you. Ethan, this I know: Holy Spirit is with you and you will know when it is time to move on, just as I know it is time for me to go on."

"Thank you" is all I can muster as the fear of the unseen future comes upon me. We part.

+ + +

Simeon has seen a rider approaching on the Jerusalem road and announces this with a yell. It is not yet the third hour so Daniel must have left early. As I round the house towards the road I see immediately that it is not Daniel on the galloping tan horse. Thaddaeus joins Simeon and me as the unknown rider arrives. His rapid breathing and the horse's heavy coat of sweat show that he has been riding hard.

"I have a message for Ethan bar Phinehas. Is this the right place?"

"I am Ethan bar Phinehas. Who sent you and what news do you bring?"

"May I dismount and lead my horse to water?"

"Yes, of course." Simeon has been joined by two armed servants. I nod for them to take care of the horse and to bring refreshments for the still unknown rider.

"Come, sit here in the shade and catch your breath. But we are anxious to hear what news you bring. This is Thaddaeus bar Alphaeus"…I almost say one of the twelve when I realize I am only assuming this unknown rider is one of us – those on 'the way.'

"Greetings, I am Amal bar Hiram." The name is common to my Mother's home around Tyre; he is probably an Asherite. " I am sent by the apostle Matthew, the former tax collector." His knowledge of Matthew's background conveys his authenticity. Knowing our anxiety for the news he goes on:

"Daniel and Caleb are safe. They are in a safe house and must move about with great care. There is danger. Since the coming of Holy Spirit in the upper room many thousands have converted to the way of Jesus the Nazarene, as I know you have." Amal glances at Thaddaeus to see if he has assumed too much. I pick up on his telling glance:

"Thaddaeus is one of the twelve", I say.

"Oh, please forgive me. I am only one of the thousands and I only know Peter and Andrew and James and John. And Matthew."

Thaddaeus interrupts, "James the brother of John?"

"Yes."

"Do you have news of my brother, James bar Alphaeus, also one of the twelve?"

"Not directly. I do know that all the twelve still in Jerusalem are safe for now. Some, like you kind sir, have left. I do not know who they are." I notice that Amal is showing real respect and deference towards Thaddaeus. The twelve must be making an impact on Jesus' disciples.

"Amal, did you see Caleb and Daniel?" I ask.

"No, but Matthew sent me to tell you they are safe. He has also sent messengers to Joseph in Arimathea and Nicodemus in Hebron."

Thaddaeus pre-empts my next inquiry: "Tell us of the danger you mentioned. What is happening now?"

"When I heard Peter speak I asked to be baptized in the Way. The twelve there baptized hundreds in a day. And hundreds more in the days to come. There was joy all over Jerusalem. All were caring for each other. No one was in need. There was rejoicing and praying throughout the city, day and night. I saw Peter heal a lame beggar. He said 'In the name of Jesus Christ the Nazarene – walk!' And Peter grabbed the beggar's arm and lifted him up. The man leaped and walked into the Temple with Peter and John – and we who were following. It was glorious."

Young Amal's face glowed; his eyes sparkled. But where was the danger?

"And then things changed?" Thaddaeus suggested.

"Yes. Peter and John were arrested and jailed by the Temple Guard. The priests and Sadducees were disturbed by Peter's preaching that day in Solomon's portico. They had informers at the meetings who reported that Peter and the apostles were preaching Jesus as the resurrected Messiah. They were chastised and released and warned not to continue proclaiming our gospel. Peter and John answered them by accusing the priests of crucifying the now risen Jesus. We were afraid they would also be crucified. But they released them, repeating the ban on preaching about Jesus. The Chief Priest was afraid of the large crowds of disciples of Jesus"

"Go on," urged Thaddaeus.

"After that many people left the streets and were afraid to be with the Apostles even though their esteem was growing. But within many households of the city, prayers and encouragement continued.

People from outside Jerusalem began to come, seeking healing and the news they heard about the risen Christ. But the priests continued to spy on us, and were afraid of an uprising."

I intercede, "What about the Romans?"

Amal replies, "That was a strange thing. There were no more than the normal Roman patrols. They did not seem to want to get involved as long as we were peaceful. And we had no reason to be otherwise. Some wondered if Pontius Pilate was having second thoughts about the wisdom of killing Jesus."

Thaddaeus muses "If only he knew that Jesus lives again."

"Is that how things stand now in Jerusalem?" I ask.

"No" continues Amal. "Peter and the Apostles continued to preach, teach, and heal. More were added to the host of believers day by day. The High Priest rose up in jealousy and anger. All of the apostles in Jerusalem were rounded up and jailed. But during the night an angel of the Lord released them and told them to go to the portico and continue to preach the gospel of Jesus." Amal is excited as he relives these marvels. "The next morning the Chief Priest assembled the Sanhedrin and sent for the apostles. I went in with a small crowd to witness this trial. It was a great shock, to me and the Council, when the guards reported that the apostles had been freed and were in the Portico preaching the forbidden. The apostles were brought in to face the Council. There were eight with Peter as the spokesman.

The Chief Priest questioned them, saying: "We gave you strict orders not to continue teaching in this name, and yet, you have filled Jerusalem with your teaching and intend to bring this man's blood upon us."

But Peter and the apostles answered, "We must obey God rather than men. The God of our fathers raised up Jesus, whom you had put to death by hanging Him on a cross. He is the one whom

God exalted to His right hand as a Prince and a Savior, to grant repentance to Israel, and forgiveness of sins. And we are witnesses of these things; and so is the Holy Spirit, whom God has given to those who obey Him."

There were shouts to "kill them" from the Council and some in the audience. But a man, a Rabbi I suppose, named Gamaliel stood and asked to speak. The apostles were removed to another room and the spectators told to leave. I do not know what the Rabbi Gamaliel said, but it was decided to flog the apostles and warn them again not to teach of Jesus."

The joy appears to drain from his countenance. "We went on rejoicing for a while, but news came that the Chief Priest and his associates were on the move again. People were harassed by the Temple Guard; some on the streets mocked us as fools; others chided us for trying to abolish the Law. Clear messages were directed to the apostles that continued disobedience would not be tolerated. There were rumors that a pogrom to eliminate the 'Way" was being planned, to be led by a fierce Pharisee, Saul of Tarsus. James, Jesus' brother, convinced the apostles to disperse in Jerusalem for now. Safe houses were found. No one knows exactly where the apostles are. James is now the spokesman for the Way.

It is now apparent that this young man was carefully chosen for this task. Amal is well spoken, very articulate. He speaks Greek as his first tongue and Aramaic next. I want to know more about him, but this is not the time.

"The dangers are grave. The priests and Sanhedrin are capable of a pogrom and I doubt the Romans would object" I offer as if Amal has concluded his report. I consider for a moment going to our Roman allies here to intervene on our behalf. But this would put our Roman friends in a possibly dangerous place. Pontius Pilate wants only an appearance of shalom through the absence of militant sects and intra-Israelite popular uprisings. I am sure he considers the Way one or the other. It is unlikely that a Roman Army subordinate would challenge Pilate. Anyway, our friendship with a few Roman authorities is only a relationship of convenience, for them and us. They care no more for our religion than we do for their religion, or absence thereof.

Amal has not finished. "There is another problem. There are now thousands of disciples in Jerusalem and they all look to the apostles to care for their souls. The apostles are exhausted. James and the twelve are discipling others but this takes time. And now that the apostles cannot move about safely the situation is even worse.

Thaddaeus says, "well of course I am returning immediately. My place is with the twelve."

Amal looks at me, "Matthew wonders if you could come and help, Ethan? He said events had overtaken his last advice for you."

This is getting more complicated by the minute. I first want to see Caleb and Daniel. I have totally unfinished business with Mother and Father. What can I do for the Way in Jerusalem? Bring some money? Yes, that I will do. What else? My mind is spinning.

I let out a soft chuckle of irony to slow my mind. Two days ago Thaddaeus and I were about to embark on an idyllic journey north and tell some sweet Jesus stories. What am I into? Where is this Way taking me!

PART FOUR

"Enough!!" I awake as if from a dream. Enough dithering. My mind is clear now about what I must do. First I must find Caleb and Daniel. Then I must find Matthew, or another of the apostles if I cannot find him. I need to know if Joseph and Nicodemus are safe – and where? What is the plan now? To my surprise I have slept late – after tossing and turning for what seemed most of the night. Thaddaeus and Amal left last evening. He thought it best to go separately for safety but I expect he was just too anxious to stay the night. I considered going with them but was still torn about Abba and Mama. The sleep cleared my mind.

"Abba, I must go to Jerusalem immediately, to find Caleb and Daniel."

"Yes, yes. I agree." Father says authoritatively.

"How is Mama?'

"She is a little ill. But we have already guessed that you would go today. We both agree. Go ahead and go. But please stay in touch with Levi so he can send messages. And be careful."

"I will. I don't how long I will be."

I arrive at Uncle Levi's office in what must be record time. Nekoda seemed to sense the urgency and galloped steadily much of the way. Levi's servant will care for him well.

"Levi, tell me what is going on here in Jerusalem. Do you have any news of Caleb and Daniel?"

"They came here to see me when they arrived from Ephraim. Let's see, that was about four or five weeks ago. Daniel came by a few times before he returned to Ephraim; Caleb came by once with Daniel a week or so ago." Uncle Levi is struggling to get his time line right. " I have not seen them since. I have made some contacts with the Sanhedrin and a Roman Centurion I know who commands the Temple area. Ethan, there is going to be trouble. Thousands have joined this "Way" of the Nazarene. Most have stopped working. People are coming in from the countryside with no place to stay, most are poor. Food will soon be a problem. The city cannot handle this. Caiaphas, the Chief Priest is under a lot of pressure – from the people and from the Romans. The Sanhedrin are his lackeys and will do his bidding. The advice of Rabbi Gamaliel was to be patient and let this pass away like other sect uprisings after the death of their leader. But this movement is different - it seems to have a power of its own. These people are more active than when their rabbi was alive! I hear that their new rabbi, Simon Peter of Galilee, is a skilled and courageous speaker and leader. He and other leaders have been jailed and released with warnings and a beating. They will surely die if they keep on flaunting the Sanhedrin. Why do this for a dead man?"

I interject: "What about Herod?"

"We hear he is away. Who knows, or cares, where." Uncle Levi does not care much for Herod. Neither do I, but I serve him.

"Ethan, what I fear is that people will take to the streets in protest. Then the Roman's will come in and there will be a bloodbath on the streets. It will be over quickly."

"I must find Caleb and Daniel. Where should I start?"

"Go to the Praetorium. You are known there. Pilate's people are trying to keep up with the potential trouble. I inquired a week ago with our contact there, Cornelius Cato, but he did not know of Daniel or Caleb. You know Cornelius. Have you met Pilate?"

"No. Father has been with him at a few functions."

Levi says: "I was with Pilate a while back in a meeting. He's a quiet fellow. Contemplative type, I'd say. A listener. When our meeting on the sewerage problems was over I thought we could do a lot worse."

I fix my eyes sharply on Levi and retort, "He crucified Jesus."

"Politics as usual for these times" Levi replies nonchalantly. "With the string of failures preceding Pilate, he knows this place can make or break his future. He cannot tolerate uprisings and threats to the appearance of peace."

"Pretty bad politics if you ask me."

"Yeah, that's why I think we are headed for a bloodbath." Levi is a bit too dispassionate.

"All right, I'll go to the Praetorium." There seem to be no other options.

+ + +

I make my way toward the Praetorium on foot, observing the people of the crowded streets. Many are lingering in small groups, others appear to be in a hurry to get somewhere. In my riding clothes I am no more noticeable than others. Levi's offices are in the carpet store down near the Old City by the Essene Gate. I walk along the wall towards Herod's Palace, then turn east to avoid running into someone I might know around the Palace. The Mishneh sector is a mish-mash of narrow alleyways lined with shops of goods from all over the world. Little chance of running into one from my crowd here. The Temple is ahead and there are many entering the Court of the Gentiles. I decide to go on to the Praetorium and as I round the Fortress of Antonia I see another crowd ahead, visibly agitated. As they make their way towards the Pool of Bethesda I hear shouts "Stone him, Kill him!!!" I cannot see the object of their derision.

A uniformed Temple Guard comes abreast and I ask: "Who are they stoning – what is going on?"

"A man named Stephen, a leader of the Jesus Way, has been seized by those of the Synagogue of the Freedmen who are determined to wipe out the Way, this Nazarene cult. Say, are you one of them – the Jesus cult?

"No!" I respond quickly, and as quickly feel a coward for it. But I do not recant the 'no'.

The guard moves on. Finally, an opening to the front of the crowd. On the crest of a hill just past the pool a large crowd is gathered, looking down at the captive Stephen, I suppose. As I crest the hill I too see the prisoner.

"NO! NO! NO!" I scream like a mad man! "THIS IS NOT STEPHEN! THIS MAN IS CALEB BAR PHINEHAS! HE IS MY BROTHER!" I bolt toward the pit where Caleb is speaking to the crowd. Three Temple Guards and another grab me and throw me to the ground. I lash out and fight to get up, yelling "CALEB! CALEB!" all the while. I cannot hear what Caleb is saying. I wonder if he hears me. I see the first stone cast. As I struggle to get free one of the Guards is over me with arm raised high. The blunt thud of a truncheon against my left temple is the last thing I remember.

+ + +

When I come to, I see Uncle Levi over me. Gradually my head begins to clear. I see Caleb's death written on Levi's face. He knows I do: "Dear Ethan, Caleb is dead."

"Yes" I say calmly. I look around to get my bearings. I am in Uncle Levi's spacious house not far from the carpet store. Edna, my quiet, shy Aunt is by Levi. As I attempt a deep breath, I clutch my right side as a terrific pain shoots through my body. I took a beating I do not remember, thank God.

"Why did they call …" before finishing the question I realize the answer. Stephanas, Stephen, his middle name. But why?

Levi finishes the question: "…call him Stephen? From what I have learned, Caleb became a Deacon, a leader among those caring for the poor and the foreigners. The Sanhedrin, or at least that snake Caiaphas and his father Annas, were after him. He was persuaded to change to Stephen to avoid capture. To be honest, I was skeptical about him reaching hero status, what with his, er, past." Levi is struggling to be respectful of Caleb. I think: from the prodigal Caleb to the martyr Stephen. Can this Jesus Way, can Holy Spirit really do such things?

Aunt Edna soothingly reports my condition. "The Doctor says you have broken ribs and bruised organs. And the concussion. You will need a long rest. He will return before nightfall." She tenderly strokes my face and I realize that part of my face is bandaged.

"But what about Caleb. We must get him back to Ephraim for a proper burial. Do Abba and Mama know?" Questions are flowing as I gain clarity.

"Relax Ethan, if you can" Levi says calmly. "You have been out for over a full day now. Let me bring you up to date. Caleb has already been buried. Our friend Joseph of Arimathea, had a peaceful place near the tomb where Jesus was laid. Of course, no one must know about this. Oh, and Joseph will visit you soon." Levi continues: "I first tried to get Caleb's body, thinking to take him home. We were not allowed to remove him from the city. Some men of the Way, very compassionate fellows, took him and buried him. And yes, I sent Jaban with the sad news to Ephraim yesterday. He has returned. Phinehas and Livia are not taking this well at all." Jaban is a bright and trusted freedman in Levi's employ whom I know and trust.

Levi continues," Jaban says Phinehas did not appear well before the news. In fact he collapsed at the sad news, but recovered. Livia is better. Jaban said she seemed to know the message before it was spoken. Daniel is there and has taken charge. All now are very anxious about you. Jaban will go again tomorrow when we know more about your injuries – and any other news."

Aunt Edna says, with unusual authority, "You must now take some food and sleep again." She cuts me off as I attempt a protest: "No more talk today. There is nothing to be done until tomorrow."

+ + +

It is now five days since Caleb's death. The headaches have slackened and my ribs and chest are still painful, but bearable. I will be well again soon enough. Jaban reports that all is as well as can be expected at Ephraim. Abba is ill and has taken to bed for complete rest. I must return as soon as possible. Thinking of riding the distance to Ephraim brings a winch – ouch! I believe three days hence will be the time to go.

Levi enters with a face bearing bad news. Is Abba all right, I wonder?

"Ethan, the pogrom to eliminate the Jesus movement is underway. Saul of Tarsus is leading it and has already arrested many of the followers. I am worried about you Ethan. I know you consider yourself one of the cult, er, Way. I have assurance from my friend Cato that you will be protected. I felt I had to go to him. I trust him. He will not betray us."

I am more concerned about Abba and Mama.

"Levi, I was thinking of three more days here. But perhaps it is time now. I must get to Mama and Abba. It will be painful to ride but I can do it. Will you have Nekoda ready by the noon hour? Can Jaban go with me?"

"I was hoping you wanted to go now. You will be safer at home. You're a brave one," Levi says with the first grin in five days. "Jaban and Nekoda are ready when you are."

The ride to Ephraim was indeed painful – and slow. There was time to share with Jaban all that had happened to me from my encounter with Jesus to the upper room to Caleb's death. He was intrigued and I urged him to make contact with some men of the Way back in Jerusalem – if there are any left. I know that many of the disciples and even most of the twelve had left because of the persecution. But surely not all.

There were also quiet times when I tried to reflect on all that happened. The pain of losing Caleb was as palpable as the pain of my injuries. Facing Abba and Mama would be hard, knowing they believed I started all this, this, what? I am stranded. I need direction. Where will it come from? This gift, called faith by Matthew, is a burden. Death and destruction have reigned these last months, not the joy of the upper room. But I do remember that joy. It is as if those tongues of fire seared my heart and sealed my soul for Jesus. I cannot fathom the mystery of Jesus but neither can I dismiss it as one of those things that pass away. I wish, I pray that I had someone, like Thaddaeus, to talk to. And where is Thaddaeus? No one knows. There is so much I want to know, to understand. Will God lift up another prophet, a communicator who can explain this gospel. Someone who can show me the good news in the midst of my despair for my lost brother, my parents. I know the pain of the Psalmist:

> *"My God, my God, why have You forsaken me?*
> *Far from my deliverance are the words of my groaning.*
> *O my God, I cry by day, but You do not answer;*
> *And by night, but I have no rest."*

PART FIVE

SIX MONTHS LATER

The funeral for Abba was two weeks ago. There were a thousand people from all over Palestine here to mourn the death of the revered ruler of Ephraim, Phinehas bar Ezer. After a very busy time with friends and relatives things were returning to normal. His death was one of those you welcome, for he had suffered from heart and lung sickness since Caleb's death. He had truly lived the proverbial full life. The long illness prepared us for his departure (to where? Eternal life?). Mama found her strength again during the time of caring for Abba. She still mourned Caleb and would now extend the mourning time to include her dear husband. She was now at peace, even with me. Thank the Lord!

I had spent many hours with Abba during his illness. I was always a little anxious that he would burden me with deathbed promises, but he never did. I am ashamed for not having understood this good man until late into his life. I saw him as a paradox. Firm as a ruler and businessman; soft as the patriarch of the noble household. Witness his grace filled welcome of his prodigal Caleb/Stephen. (So many have come to pay their respects to Caleb's family who knew him as Stephen that we often call him by both names.) Abba was truly a graceful man. Forgiving of spirit, generous with all, kind. A lovely man; and my Abba. He never asked me anything about the future. I came to realize he trusted me to do the right thing. He knew I would. Will I?

+ + +

The intensity of the pogrom was short lived, but effective. Many were arrested, many imprisoned, many flogged, but few killed. Most of the Israelites of the Way fled Jerusalem, or were forced to leave. The apostles have all returned safely and remain in Jerusalem. Saul of Tarsus, leader of the pogrom, disappeared. There are many rumors: that he was ambushed on the way to Damascus; that he is a captive in Damascus; that he fled back to his home in Tarsus. Whatever happened, when he disappeared the force went out of the pogrom and things are returning to somewhat normal.

I have visited the city several times. I now know all of the apostles. Thaddaeus and I resumed our friendship and he is a powerful witness for Jesus, especially with his stories. Peter and young John have emerged as leaders of the apostles. James, the brother of Jesus has become a sort of moderator for the apostles. He also is skilled in dealing with the Sanhedrin and the Romans when necessary.

Matthew has become my spiritual director. He is very interested in the philosophy and theology of the Way of Jesus, the Messiah. Matthew has opened my eyes to the richness of the ancient scriptures as they prophesy to the coming of Jesus the Messiah. I have spent some time with the others, which they seem glad to give. That lamentful day on the road home after Caleb/Stephen's stoning has faded. I have become much stronger in my faith. We do not discuss my future, or, for that matter, anyone's future. For Jesus said:

"So do not worry about tomorrow; for tomorrow will care for itself. Each day has enough trouble of its own." But I have been planning, silently, for my future. It is all very clear to me now.

+ + +

"Mother, we need to talk." My formal address caused Mama's eyebrow to rise.

"Now is a good time." She turns toward the window where the colors of the Fall season spill into the room. I pause to read her mood. She is pensive or perhaps resigned to the inevitability of another burden to bear. Her face, in the radiance of the setting sun, shows signs of rapid aging during these hard times; but she retains her unique elegance, her privileged bearing, her lingering beauty.

"Mama, will you tell me of what you are thinking about your, our, future?" There is no point in not getting to the point. Mama is an intelligent planner and I know she has given thought to the future.

"Ethan, I have given the future much thought. But it comes down to what you intend to do. Shall you assume your Father's mantle and continue the traditional way? If so, my life choice is simple. Shall you abandon your inheritance and follow another way?" She paused before the last 'way' for emphasis that was not necessary. "If so, everyone's life here becomes vey complicated." She fixes her eyes on mine, and we look deeply into one another.

"You know I am committed to Jesus the Christ as the Lord of my life." (Perhaps using the Greek Christ will be less challenging than saying Messiah.) "And I am also committed to you and my family. I hope you know that."

"Yes Ethan, I know you are. Over these difficult months you, and Daniel, have been more loving, more compassionate than I could expect. You are much more settled with your inner self. I find nothing to condemn in this Jesus Way, at least on a personal level."

"And on other levels?"

"Family, the traditions of our Hebrew community. Those are the levels that concern me. You are more committed to your Way than to our way." She continues to emphasize 'Way' mockingly.

"It is not My Way, Mama."

"Is it not? Do you not see that you are doing what Caleb did, only with a different destination, I presume? Will you really care about those left behind, any more than Caleb did? Can you explain to me why this choice is not simply selfish?"

I pause as my thoughts go to Jesus' prophesy that the sharp edge of His gospel would sometimes divide and not unite. "He who loves father and mother more than me is not worthy of me" Jesus said. Oh Lord, this is too hard a saying. Why, oh why, cannot we have both, the old way and the new way!

Finally I say, "If I am selfish I will be condemned. The essence of the gospel is unselfishness. Jesus said we are to deny our self, and live for the other."

"Deny your self? Ethan you are in denial, denial of your selfishness!"

"Mother, you may be right, God forbid. But this I know: my encounter with Jesus left a mysterious hold on my mind; the power of Holy Spirit came over me and I was changed in that moment; I have witnessed the miracles of the apostles; witnesses to Jesus' crucifixion and resurrection are still among us; my brother was overtaken by the same Spirit and became a saint of love and caring. Jesus has hold of me and I cannot turn away."

"So you have decided to go your own way, the Jesus way."

"No, I have not decided. I have prayed for a way to follow Jesus and provide for the continued success of the estate. I believe God has shown me the way."

"And what is this way, yet another way?" Mama asks, sarcastic and skeptical.

"Mama, do you really want to spend the rest of your days here in Ephraim, or would returning to Tyre be more appealing."

"I have thought about that. Home in Tyre is certainly appealing if you leave here. But what happens to the estate here? Daniel cannot buy it and I am not sure he can manage it."

"Daniel would be pleased to continue to serve under another."

"And who might this other be?" Mama says, eyes alert.

Now for my plan, no, my vision.

"Seth." I reply.

Mama raises one eyebrow at this. "Seth?" she repeats. "Your 'twin' cousin?"

"Yes Mama, Seth. He has proved his mettle for stewarding and politics in Tyre. Seth has become the chief family diplomat with the Sanhedrin, Romans, and Phoenicians. If he can deal with those in Tyre, Ephraim will be a breeze. With Daniel at his side the household of Phinehas bar Ezer will continue to prosper. And he is the second son in Tyre. It is not unprecedented for such a relative to succeed to head of another household in certain circumstances. Within the family, of course."

"Certain circumstances indeed!" Mama says forcefully. But I can sense she is intrigued. She continues, "Why are you so confidant that my family will agree to this?"

"I'm not. I have spoken to no one, no one about this. And if you do not agree this will go no further."

"So, as they say in Tyre, the ball is now in my court." Mama is difficult to be pinned down. "Ethan, let's say Seth and the family agree. Would you convey all of the estate, your estate now, to Seth?"

"Convey? If you mean without compensation, no. I expect them to pay full value. I am sure they would insist on that."

"I'm not. You do not know us Tyreans as well as you think. Why would you want the money if you are going to be a beggar on your Way." She continues to needle me.

"Full value. That is the only way." My resolve puzzles her. "Mama, sleep on it."

After sleeping on it for a few days, Mother had agreed to approach her family with the proposal. Seth was very receptive and other key members of the family were amenable to exploring the offer. They were, of course, befuddled about me. However, the Jesus movement had come to Phoenicia and Tyre. They were becoming accustomed to 'strange' changes in people. Daniel was a key to the deal because his business acumen complemented Seth's more public persona. The Hebrew mercantile model usually relied on a team of outside and inside managers. Daniel was wholly supportive because he had found a way to serve the Lord here in Ephraim. He was as convinced that his calling was to stay here as I was convinced that mine was to leave.

Mother and I traveled to Tyre where she stayed during the talks. I returned and made one more journey there for final agreement. Seth and other family members spent considerable time here as they did their evaluation and due diligence. The bargaining was interesting. At first, as Mama had predicted, Seth assumed this was a distressed sale and a very good outcome would be his. The desire of Mother's family to extend their Tyrean empire into the heart of Palestine balanced my desire to sell. They were surprised at my hard stance on 'full value'. Not a dinar less and not a dinar more. When the valuation began to get to a level that threatened the sale, Uncle Levi came to the rescue. He could afford to buy out the Jerusalem stores, which eased the Tyrean clan's burden. The Tyreans were not merchants. Ship building and agriculture was their forte so Levi's offer would make the transition easier as well as less costly.

The lawyers tried to extend the process but it was soon clear that a motivated seller and buyer, despite being family, could come to terms amicably. Seth and his people came last week to meet with me and my people to seal the deal. A very considerable sum now awaits my withdrawal in our Jerusalem bank.

+ + +

Nekoda, not part of the sale, strides easily towards Jerusalem. I get Levi to accompany me to the bank as a witness. The banker knows us well, indeed as he should, since we have been a major depositor for many years. He is trustworthy and sanctioned by the Romans, a very important distinction. The transaction takes only a short time.

We make our way to the house by the Essene Gate – the same house where Holy Spirit came. In this now more peaceful time, the apostles rented it and the upper room was now the center for the Way. James, Jesus' brother and the moderator with the apostles, awaits my coming at a prearranged time.

"Welcome Ethan, Levi." James is a rather nondescript man of medium stature. Though younger than Jesus he appears older than my recollection of Jesus. Thaddaeus and Matthew join us on the way to the stairs. After hugs and greetings we reach the upper room.

James begins: "Ethan, we have heard much of you from Thaddaeus and Matthew. We are all blessed to have you on the Way with us." He turns toward Levi, " And Levi, we know of your fine reputation as a merchant in Jerusalem. Welcome to you both. Gentlemen, how may we be of service to you?"

Neither James nor the apostles know what I am about to do.

"Kind Sirs, this is a certificate of deposit at the Jerusalem Bank, now in your name Brother James. This is my tithe to the Lord. I only request that it be given to the poor as you see fit. I give this to God in honor of my dear brother Caleb/Stephen, who served the poor and died for their sake."

James did not appear to be surprised at the amount of the gift. I am sure it was more money than these holy peasants could imagine, even Matthew the ex-tax collector.

"Ethan, this is an answered prayer for we have great need among the poor and the widows. Please rest assured that this will go to the poor in honor of Deacon Stephen, Caleb, who devoted his last days to caring for them."

"Now, Brother Thaddaeus, as the close friend of Brother Ethan, please pray."

Thaddaeus nodded but, in character, paused for a long while. He looked at me and before lowering his head, a slight smile creased his lips. "I pray the words of the prophet Hosea:

"Sow with a view to righteousness,
Reap in accordance with kindness;
Break up your fallow ground,
For it is time to seek the LORD
Until He comes to rain righteousness on you. Amen."

There could have been no better prayer for this time than this revival of Hosea. That simple short verse was the sum of my life since that first encounter with Jesus. After goodbyes Levi and I were on the street where the crowds once yelled 'they are drunk!' Drunk indeed!

As I look back over this holy city I realize I am at the mid point between Golgotha and the Bethesda Pool. On my right, my Savior Jesus died for our sins. On my left, my mysterious brother Caleb/Stephen died for our courage to follow Jesus.

I turn back toward the gate. Levi says "Come back and rest awhile and collect Nekoda and lets talk about what is next for you."

Levi is concerned for this once rich young ruler now a mendicant without a copper coin to his name.

"No Levi, Nekoda is my gift to you for your constant love and assistance. I'll be walking – and I'll be fine."

"Ethan, where will you go?"

"I hear there is a church forming in Antioch of Syria. I shall go there. I can stop at Tyre to be with Mother awhile. Goodbye dear Levi, perchance we will meet again."

"Goodbye Ethan. And God bless you."

After a few steps I look back. Nekoda had stopped and turned his head and his large, soulful eyes were fixed on me. Uncle Levi stood still for this sacred last parting of master and stallion. With a wave and a smile, we part - forever – or does eternal life portend a reunion? Nekoda is the only thing I considered a real sacrifice as I shed my wealth.

I stride through the gate, joyful with a song in my heart: "Free at last, free to follow Jesus." What once haunted me now delights me: **"One thing you still lack: sell all that you possess and distribute it to the poor, and you shall have treasure in heaven; and come, follow Me."**

Jesus knew.

THE END

SIT FINIS LIBRI, NON FINIS QUAERENDI
(From Thomas Merton)

SHORT STORIES for the
SEASONS of the CHURCH

ADVENT	1) Zacharias
	2) Christmas with Joseph
LENT	The Leper
EASTER	Working on the Sabbath (Thaddaeus' Story)
ASCENSION	Settling on Ascension – A Poem
PENTECOST	Upstairs
ORDINARY TIME	Boating with Jesus

ZACHARIAS

Luke 1

My daily meditations are still fixed on that amazing day in Temple, now almost six months past. What started out as another routine ritual of the burning of the incense that Sabbath has certainly turned out to be anything but routine. Is this a dream or is it really happening? Why is this happening to me? I think that I should somehow be beyond these still elementary meditation questions. Why, after six months, am I still asking, "Why me?"

Who am I, really? I had been a priest at the Temple for a long time. One of several minor priests serving at the Temple. I am growing old, now in my 61st year. My dreams and ambitions of becoming the Chief Priest have been put away. I really believe I have long been at peace with where God has placed me. My envy of others who moved ahead of me in the priestly order is only a distant memory. I am aware that I have gained a respected reputation as an elder among the people and even my peers in the priesthood. I know that many say, "now Zacharias is a righteous and blameless priest". It is sad that they cannot say that about all the priests. Oh, they don't seem to notice my private sins, or if they do they are very gracious and kind to overlook my weaknesses. Rather, they honor my ability to perform the sacred rituals decently and in order. They seem to respect me for my vow to live a simple life with Elizabeth, my loving and faithful wife, my great gift from God. In mid-life I came to peace with my limitations and my vow to follow the advice of the prophet Micah: love kindness, do justice, and walk humbly with God.

Even as I acknowledge my good repute among the people, I recognize the shallowness of my faith; my inner struggle to see beyond the worship rituals, to behold the true glory of God. But I do desire to glorify God, and I believe that God honors that desire. I can only hope and pray that God forgives and forgets those times when I allow the wanderings of my mind, my slothfulness, to reduce my worship to ritual only. Forgives those times when only my mind and not my heart are present at the altar. I renew my vow to follow Micah's rule, to righteously obey the law as best I can, and strive against sin. Elizabeth is my real inspiration. Where my faith is weak, hers' is strong. If I envy anyone, it is Elizabeth, for her faith in God seems to come easy to her. She is comfortable in her faith, not restless like me. Ah well, I shall continue to pray for a greater portion of faith and thank God that he has given me a wife of strong faith.

I have now accepted, on faith, that it really was Gabriel, the Lord's angel, who came to me that day in the Temple. The events that have followed are real enough. Elizabeth, nearly fifty, is pregnant for the first time. I am mute now for these six months. The shallowness of faith I displayed in that moment of Gabriel's appearance distresses me even now as I recall the startling scene. Insisting on proof that he was Gabriel the angel! Oh Lord I believe, help my unbelief! I see dimly now the wisdom of striking me mute. This great thing that is unfolding - the coming of our son who will announce the coming of the Messiah - must somehow happen in the fullness of time according to God's plan. This is no time for a weak-willed priest prone to speaking before thinking to complicate things.

I realize that being mute has been a blessing. Oddly, these six months have been rather peaceful. I am now honorably retired from my Temple position, and I was ready for that. I have discovered a new way to pray in my enforced silence, and in this new way I have experienced the presence of God's spirit as I never did before. This new way must surely be a gift of God. I read Scripture, especially the Psalms, I meditate on the reading, I pray, and in my silence I wait for the Lord to visit my soul. In my sacred readings, I have searched out the prophesies of the Messiah. Through my meditations on these Scriptures, my prayers, and my time of waiting in silence, I know deep in my heart that the promise of Gabriel is true. John my son will be born in a few months, and Messiah will follow. When will He come? How will we know Him? Where will He come from? Speculations flood my mind. Stop, Zacharias, my heart seems to say. Be silent, wait. One of the readings from the Psalter comes into my consciousness:

> *Wait for the LORD;*
> *Be strong and let your heart take courage;*
> *Yes, wait for the LORD.*

I am able to obey as I reckon this to be the very word that God wants me to hear. I am able to brake my hyperactive mind. I pray again for added portions of faith that I know will be needed to wait on the Lord. Another sacred reading is spoken by the Spirit into my consciousness:

> *Sow with a view to righteousness,*
> *Reap in accordance with kindness;*
> *Break up your fallow ground, For it is time to seek the LORD*
> *Until He comes to rain righteousness on you*

I am filled with a sense of peace, I know the Lord has met me again in the contemplation of his Holy word. My soul rejoices in the hope of the Lord. Praise the Lord!

But now, I must prepare to receive Elizabeth's niece Mary from over at Nazareth. Mary has sent word that she has some important family news and Elizabeth seems excited about it.

FINIS

CHRISTMAS WITH JOSEPH

Matt 1:18-25

It is now the eighth day of the journey from Nazareth to Bethlehem for the Roman census. Our group of twelve left Nazareth to register in the towns of our families' origins. Eleazar and his family only had to travel to Tiberius, while the rest of us trekked down to the Jordan River valley to Jericho, Jerusalem, and Bethany. My hometown, Bethlehem, the city of David, was the furthest south. Our dear friends, Samuel and Samantha, were the last of the group to leave us, at Bethany.

Samuel was very concerned that we would arrive too late in Bethlehem to find a room, for the entire route was filled with travelers like us going to register for Caesar's census and the inns were often filled. But we had managed to find accommodations along the way and I was hopeful that Bethlehem would not be so crowded. We discovered that others going to Bethlehem were staying in Jerusalem and would make a day trip to Bethlehem to register. I suggested we stay in the Jerusalem where Mary could rest and be with friends while I went on down to Bethlehem, but Mary insisted on coming with me. The sun is setting and I can see Bethlehem ahead. We should arrive within the hour.

Mary has awakened from her nap in the wagon. The road is well traveled and smooth from Bethany to Bethlehem and Pokey, our donkey, is able to strike a steady pace allowing enough comfort for Mary to doze off. She has become very tired after a week of walking and rough cart riding. A rare occasion for a quiet and a gentle ride for her.

"Mary, how are you feeling now?"

"I'm fine. I am sure you are exhausted though. You have walked for how many days now? And I ride like a princess. I'll rub your feet when we get to the inn." Mary seems refreshed.

"That sounds like heaven on earth, I'll go faster!" I'm very tired but try to match Mary's cheerfulness.

"Giddy up, Pokey!" Mary laughs out. Pokey is not into this conversation and continues his steady but leisurely pace.

Turning back to look at her, seriously I say, "Mary, I'm worried that the baby will come early, before we get home"

"Elizabeth says the baby is a month away, and she knows about these things", Mary says too confidently. Mary's Aunt Elizabeth had given birth to John just a few months ago. She was also a midwife. Long after giving up hope of having her own baby, she had characteristically turned to help others. Then, past her time, she bore little John. She has been very close to Mary through their pregnancies, both as a loving aunt and a midwife caring for Mary - and me.

"And whatever Aunt Elizabeth says has got to be so, eh?", my seriousness giving way to an attempt at sarcasm. Mary lets it pass, knowing I mean no harm. She knows I love and respect Aunt Elizabeth and Uncle Zacharias, for they are both wise and love us very much. Besides, they are the only others who are in on this thing that is about to happen.

My mind goes back to the memories of the events around Mary becoming pregnant. Memories of shock and anger and embarrassment when she became pregnant during our betrothal time. We had followed custom and not had sex during the betrothal. Her explanation for her pregnancy shortly before the marriage ceremony was unbelievable! I was within my rights to dismiss her, to send her away. I was crushed, for I truly loved Mary. She was all a man could hope for in a wife - kind, affectionate, intelligent, and beautiful. She was also known for her modesty, loyalty, and truthfulness - hardly a candidate for an adulteress. Yet adultery was the only reasonable explanation. But then three forces came together to persuade me that Mary's story was true. First, the goodness of her character defied her apparent sin - no matter what the evidence, it did not ring true. Then the powerful dream of the angel which was so like Mary's story of her encounter with the angel. Finally, the belief and faith of Aunt Elizabeth and Uncle Zacharias that their John would announce the coming of the Messiah, our Jesus. Uncle Zacharias' visit by the angel Gabriel was so much like my dream, and like Mary's remembrance of the angel that to call them coincidences defied belief. Somehow, I came to accept this wondrous prophecy, although I do not know how. Uncle Zacharias' letters and his encouraging talks, when he got his voice back after John was born, brought me back from the depths of doubt many times. His basic message is that God has given us a capacity for faith, hope, and love that far exceeds what our minds can grasp. Well, what I have accepted as true about the lovely girl with the baby in her womb in the cart behind me certainly is beyond what this feeble mind can grasp. Somehow, my heart can grasp it. Uncle Zach calls it faith.

We arrive at the inn in Bethlehem just as darkness settles in. The inn doesn't look promising. There are men crowded in the lobby, some already drunk. I explain our situation to the innkeeper, pointing to Mary sitting awkwardly in the cart outside. The innkeeper is sympathetic, but the inn is filled beyond capacity.

"You would not want to bring your wife into this mess of a place anyway", he says compassionately. " I just had my private stable cleaned and it is more private. I can give you some bedding and with the straw and animals close by it should be warm enough. I can send out some food and water." I accept immediately. The inns on the way here did not rise above the level of a recently cleaned stable. Somebody ought to do something about the sorry state of inns.

The stable was indeed clean and warm. After arranging the bedding and returning from the inn with some food, I find Mary lying down. She is pale and not looking well at all.

"Mary, I thought you were feeling well? You do not look well."

"Joseph, I believe labor pains have started", she says rather matter of factly. "I have had some little pains since yesterday, but I really didn't think they were labor pains. I didn't want to worry you. I think Auntie was off a little on the timing." Mary is stressed but unafraid.

I take a deep breath and resist the urge to panic. Aunt Elizabeth had prepared me for just this moment in case Jesus decided to come without proper advance notice (That's good, Joseph, try to keep your humor about you, I think to myself). I know how to deliver a baby. No, as Aunt Elizabeth said, you do not deliver a baby; you receive a baby, like you receive a gift.

"Mary, let's pray." We both ask God to be with us and to guide us. After the prayer, one thing is clear. I will deliver, no, receive baby Jesus myself. Mary agrees. I get some water and cloths and prepare a crib in the just scrubbed manger. I sit beside her, take her hand, and wait. The two burros and the two goats are quiet and radiating warmth. I begin to have thoughts of the absurdity of this: 'Immanuel, God with us, being born as a human baby in a barn! Joseph, I scold myself, faith in God has brought you to this place, now finish the race set before you!'

The pains are coming regularly now, but Mary remains calm even as she begins to really labor. After about an hour, the water breaks, and baby Jesus comes. I receive him, this bewildering, amazing gift of God. Wiping the blood and afterbirth away I behold a wrinkled, tiny baby boy, crying vigorously, and wondering if he can be anyone other than just my boy. Mary, glowing with relief and love receives Jesus and tenderly enfolds him to her bosom. Jesus and Mary are quiet and at peace together. So am I. Mary reaches out to me and enfolds me also to her bosom. The three of us are as one.

After a while I take Jesus from his now sleeping mother and hold him in my lap. As I gaze down at the sleeping baby Jesus, I am startled by a new thought. I am to be this child's Father! During the pregnancy I was so occupied with the enormity of the conception and the meaning of all this that I had not thought about actually being a father to this baby. How does one be a father to the Son of God. For the first time this glorious night, I am afraid. I am really afraid. I pray for the angel to return and tell me to fear not! To tell me how to be a father to the Son of God. The angel does not come. I sink into the depths of this enormous tidal wave that has engulfed my life. Jesus stirs and whimpers. I begin to think of his needs, not mine. This is time for a lullaby. I begin to sing softly:

Mary are you sleeping?
Mary I'm afraid
Mary can I live up to the choice that God has made?
Jesus can you tell me, here upon my knee,
What kind of father will I be?
What can I give to You,
You, made from miracles
That God has given me to keep?
I can't give much to You, You made of miracles,
But I can hold You as You sleep.
What can You learn from me; You, made from miracles;
When I've so much to learn from You?
What can a man like me offer the miracle
Who taught me that miracles come true.
Tell me how to guide You, Tell me what to say,

Tell me how to show You how to show the world the Way;
How to please the angels, watching from above
When all I have to give You is love.
But if it's love You need, You, made from miracles
Then take my hand and hold it tight, and I will give You love.
Sweet, little miracle that God has given me tonight
Sweet little miracle, Oh, what a miracle
That God has given us tonight.

Finis

THE LEPER

Mark 1:40-45

The glory of the early Fall morning is a cruel irony. The ugliness of my body, deformed as it is with leprosy, is but magnified by the beauty of the day. The sun's rising light defines the symmetry and the perfect blending of texture and color in the countryside. Even the sweet decaying smells of the soil are in perfect harmony with the fading colors of the trees. The day's glory is complete with the music of the birds, a symphony of sound now with the mockingbird's solo accentuated by the cymbalic honks of the geese on the lake. How frivolous, how random, how sad it all seems. The beautiful and the ugly side by side, created by the whimsy of uncaring nature, and if there is one, an uncaring God.

If there is one...? If there is the God of our Fathers and he punishes the sinful as we have been taught then I deserve my leprosy. I was a great sinner, a mocker of God and his followers. How simple it was to twist the law of those fools and disturb their belief. Where was God when your baby died? Where was your faith when you had the adulterous affair? How easy it was to mock others when I was young and healthy. Then the horror of leprosy. The priest whom I mocked was openly gleeful when he pronounced to the village that God had his revenge and my sins were the cause of my affliction. I don't mock God or his followers any more. Even here in the leper colony Yahweh has his followers. Gomer is an old woman who has been a leper since she was a child, yet she has a joy about her that she says comes from faith in Yahweh. Jotham spends all his time and energy caring for those who are sick. He says Yahweh loves the poor and the sick and therefore he does also. Jotham is always quoting the Prophet Micah and saying that leprosy has its blessings in that it is easier to love kindness, do justice, and walk humbly with God in our little band of horrors. I understand the humble part, but where is the justice and kindness? I see it in Gomer and Jotham, but not in the God they worship.

My daily melancholy now fully engaged, I begin to think about the rumor of a new Rabbi preaching in these parts. They say he has a new message of forgiveness and healing. As my cynicism is about to take over and muse about how I've heard it all before, Jotham comes over to me.

"Ahaz, I want you to go and see this Rabbi, Jesus from Nazareth. I promised to sit with Uzziah today - I think he will die any time now and I want to be here when his time comes. Bring me news of what he has to say."

"Jotham, I wouldn't be able to get close enough to get a good look at him, much less hear what he has to say." Jotham eyes me studiously for a moment. "Ahaz, you have many faults, and being a messenger of hope might be a stretch for you, but you are bold, and if anyone here could get close to him it would be you." Jotham was kind and also blunt.

" Well, I had big plans today, but anything for a friend. That's what I always say." Jotham ignored or missed my sarcasm.

"He will be at the synagogue in Magdala this afternoon. You had better get started."

Hiding my disfigured face and hands with hood and robe and walking off the side of the road as required, I begin the one hour walk into Magdala from our colony to the south. The coolness of the Fall day and scarce encounters with other people on the road make for a tolerable walk. I find myself with a sense of adventure, even excitement, instead of the normal gloom of melancholy that usually accompanies me. I begin to think how I will maneuver my way close enough to hear him without being shunned and turned away. I once brazenly walked into a crowd and felt like Moses before the Red Sea as the people receded before me. But the punishment imposed for that caper persuades me not to attempt that again. One more hill with the view of the Sea to the east and I'll be there.

At the top of the hill a road converges from the west and the steep slope on both sides forces me to walk almost on the road. A rather large group - there must be twenty or so men and women - comes onto the road into Magdala, coming within a few feet of me. Their talking subsides as they cast cautious glances at me and try to move away. But the size of the group and the lay of the road forces us closer.

Someone says -glancing at me - to a young man towards the front of the group: "We must hurry for the crowds are waiting." He is more concerned about getting away from me than their arrival in the village. The young man turns back as if to answer, but I feel his eyes on me. I glance his way, and yes, he is looking at me. There is no fear or disgust in his eyes. He has the eyes of Gomer and Jotham. Kind eyes. Then the man addresses him again, "Jesus, we must hurry!" "This is Jesus!", I think to myself. "I cannot get closer than this!"

What happened in the next moments are almost a blur. I found myself on my knees at Jesus feet shouting "If you are willing, you can make me clean." I am looking into those kind eyes, those compassionate eyes. Even as the others move away from us in shock, Jesus reaches out and touches my face - my gnarled, infested face.

"I am willing; be cleansed."

I immediately see that my hands are clean and restored to their youthful strength. I can feel the changes to my face and see fully out of my left eye that had been partially swollen shut from the beginning of the leprosy. Am I really cured? Jesus is saying something to me but

I cannot concentrate. " ... to a priest...Moses commanded..." I cannot hear him now for the shouts of the crowd now drawn closer around me. He seems to be telling me to go. I want to say something but no words come. I must really be clean! I must go and ask someone.

I bolt from the crowd and run back toward the colony. Another group approaches and I shout to them that Jesus the Nazarene has cleansed me from leprosy. Yes, you are clean they assure me. Everyone must know this man Jesus who heals even sinners such as me! Everyone must know! I shall shout it from the rooftops. Glory, Alleluia, I was a leper and now I am clean. Surely Jesus is the Messiah. All must know.

It is almost two weeks since Jesus healed me. I had heard that he is in Capernaum. I have made the day's journey from our colony to try to see him and thank him. The trek along the Sea road has been a joy, without the soreness and discomfort that would have been with me before my healing. There is a large crowd in the village. I approach a group gathered around the well in the village center talking about Jesus healing a man who had been paralyzed for many years. People pay no attention to me as I edge my way into the group to hear more. I savor the lack of attention that my now ordinary appearance evinces. "Where is Jesus now?", I ask no one in particular.

"He's at home resting", says a rather stern young man.

"Can I see him? He healed me of leprosy a couple of weeks back and I want to thank him."

"Oh, it's you", said the stern young man, becoming even more stern. "You are the reason he's worn out and needs to rest. He asked you to tell no one about the healing but you evidently told everyone in East Galilee!" The young man seems a little angry at me.

"And who might you be?", I ask, annoyed.

"I am Judas Iscariot, one of the twelve with Jesus. Look, we have important work to do," failing in his attempt at gentler tone. "These healings are necessary to gain support for the revolt he will lead, but there have been enough and he needs to rest." This is an intense fellow! I had heard the rumors that Jesus is the Messiah who would lead the revolt against the Romans.

I am more annoyed, "Maybe I am just a tool for some cockeyed plot against the Roman's, but I was a leper and now am healed! People must know about one who can heal sinners!" I realize I am almost shouting at Judas. The crowd backs away from us. I think they are hoping for a fight.

"What's going on?", a voice from behind me asks. Without turning, I recognize Jesus' voice. "What's the matter, Judas." His voice is calm and I sense that the budding argument with Judas is already over as he comes between us.

"This is that leper you healed down in Magdala", Judas replies dutifully, the anger gone.

"Oh, it's you, Ahaz", Jesus says behind those same soft eyes I had looked into that first meeting.

"You know my name?", I ask, genuinely surprised.

"How could I not? You were thankful for your healing, but you don't seem to follow directions very well do you?" He was not perturbed - his attitude was rather playful.

"What do you mean?", I ask, honestly.

"Well, I had a pretty full schedule for the next several days." Jesus glanced at Judas with a knowing smile. Judas' head dropped perceptibly as he fixed his eyes on Jesus. Their looks belied some matter of tension between them. "Judas here and some of my other friends are in a hurry about some things, and you seemed to be very efficient at spreading good news. We were overrun with people everywhere and your name came up a lot." His attention is fully on me, the pointed banter with Judas over now. The two of us are now the center of attention as the crowd has grown.

"I just wanted to thank you", I say, meekly. "This is a great thing you did for me. Did you know that I have been a great sinner and a mocker of Yahweh?" Was this a foolish risk? I realize that he could probably recall the leprosy.

"You were?", he asks. I feel fear rising as I recall the horror of leprosy. Then I realize that his reply was rhetorical. "But what are you now?" I see by his eyes that this is a serious question and he awaits a serious reply.

"The cords of death were around me, the terrors of Hell were upon me, I was in distress

and sorrow. When I called upon you to save my life, you heard me and you saved me. You are my Lord and Messiah. I will always love you. I will always be your servant. I will always sing your praises in the presence of all the people."

Jesus looks at me approvingly. "You have been meditating on the Psalms. Well done good and faithful servant." Jesus turns, motions for Judas, and walks towards his house.

I turn towards my home. What lies ahead for Jesus, for me? I don't know; but I know it is time to begin a new journey.

Finis

WORKING on the SABBATH
(THADDAEUS' STORY)

Mark 3:1-6

I am a Pharisee. I am one of the group who has just witnessed Jesus from Nazareth illegally heal a man on the Sabbath. I am an accepted Holy man of my community, an honorable and respected church leader. This man, Jesus, has been attacking my group's legitimacy as the spiritual leaders of our people. Yet we are the ones who have been true and faithful to our long traditions of faith. We are the true followers of Yahweh. It is we who have labored long and hard to faithfully perfect the Law of Moses. It is we who have codified the Laws of Moses clearly and explicitly so that the people can understand and obey. God will surely honor our efforts to strictly adhere to the letter of the Law which Yahweh gave to our Fathers, even the great Moses.

Our cadre gathers outside to meet with the agents of Herod assigned to investigate the disturbances caused by Jesus and his followers. My anger is growing inside me as I think about the abomination that just happened in the synagogue. Aaron, the true Rabbi here, reminds us of our fealty to the Law of God and our duty to expose pretenders and heretics. The Herodians are exclaiming about the growing potential for civic unrest that will surely bring down the wrath of the Romans to the harm of us all. My thoughts are squarely on this man Jesus, an uneducated peasant carpenter from Nazareth (indeed, can anything good come from Nazareth?), who flaunts his pretentious claim to be a Rabbi. This Jesus who mocks the laws of the Sabbath! This Jesus has violated the Law by healing the withered hand right here in the synagogue, the very house of the Lord! Rabbi Seth reminds us that Jesus not only healed the man but he had the audacity to become angry at us for trying to protect the Law! I wonder what provoked his anger? Was it our refusal to answer his simplistic question about doing good on the Sabbath? How could one of his lowly state understand the complexity of the Law which in this case supersedes his desire to do apparently random acts of kindness.

The discussion has turned heated and some are arguing that his violations are serious enough for legal action. Some suggest capital punishment. But as this discussion continues, I notice the peasant whose hand was healed leaving the synagogue with his friends and family. They are overjoyed and amazed that the once grotesquely disfigured hand is restored. He jabs his arm into the air repeatedly and opens and clinches his healed hand and shouts hosannas to the exiting crowd. He is truly joyful and is obviously untroubled by the violation of the Law. Will he ever repent. Will he realize that God can bring upon him far greater affliction than a withered hand for his disobedience. Does he not consider the wrath of God that has been visited upon our people in the past for our disobedience of the Law? Does he not consider the curse of God we are under now - the oppression of the Romans that make these Herodian agents mere puppets of Pontius Pilate? Does he think that life is as simple as just being healed? Woe to you, Jesus and your victims!

But my heart is restless within me. I cannot put the joy of the healing out of my mind. I am disturbed that my training and upbringing to strive to be obedient to the law is challenged by this Galilean and his healing. I cannot escape the haunting question that I know is on the mind of many of us: if he is not of God, how can he do these things? Our leaders say he practices sorcery by the power of Satan. Perhaps. I have remained uncharacteristically silent during the discussions, preoccupied by my own thoughts and doubts. I feel a strong desire to know more about Jesus of Nazareth.

As our group leaves, I slip away to question Jesus. I find him in a small olive grove by the well with two of his followers. They do not yet see me. After a drink of water, he sits silently in his own thoughts or perhaps waiting for someone. I decide to take this opportunity and address him without introduction.

"How can you transgress the law of the Sabbath, even for a good deed?" I am somewhat chagrined by my confronting attitude, but wonder why I am concerned about being polite to this pretender. He lifts his gaze to me slowly and calmly, not responding for what seems like a long while.

"Our Father, Yahweh, Abba, loves beyond the law", he answers softly, matter of factly. His utterance of the Father as Abba startles me. No one in their right mind would address Yahweh the way a child would address their earthly father. But I know from his countenance that this man is not out of his mind. In fact, I sense an authentic authority in his voice. Pausing as if to give me time to size him up, he then continues. "You are a leader among the Pharisees, and you are right to love the law." Again he pauses as if to allow me to silently acknowledge that he is right on both counts. Our eyes are now met, and I wonder where he is going with this, feeling no need to respond.

"You have lost your first love, the love of your Father, Abba, for the love of the pursuits of your own minds." Now he seems to wait for a response. But I am silent in the realization that duty, not love, is my watchword. The shame of being outwitted by a Galilean peasant flits through my mind but recedes as I see the tenderness in his eyes..

"What is your name", he asks? "Joseph, Joseph Barsabbas", I reply.

"Joseph, my Father's name", Jesus replies. "Ah, but 'Joseph Barsabbas', son of the Sabbath". He smiles, "No wonder you are devoted to the laws of the Sabbath." His tone is ironic, but kind. I wonder about why I seem content to let him speak and to not respond. The animosity I carried has dissipated.

"Joseph Barsabbas", he says compassionately, "you know in your heart that love is the true foundation of the law, that the Sabbath is meaningless without the love and grace of our heavenly Father. Joseph Barsabbas, you know in your heart that love is greater than your laws." He says my name as from one with authority over me. I am perplexed.

"Surely you are not the Messiah as some say?", I hear myself asking.

He smiles again, but does not answer. Rather he rises and turns to leave.

Then he turns back to me.

"Come, follow me."

I follow him.

Finis

SETTLING on ASCENSION

The lake by the Monastery is still,
Still here in the early evening
Here by the lake on Ascension's Eve.

There is no sign of Ascension.
Things are descending, settling, not ascending.
Things, things like ducks, geese, butterflies.

Things like me?
Settling for the night, all descending
Here by the Monastery's still waters.

Is there any sign of the Ascension promised tomorrow?
A fish ascends from the deep to shatter the still waters;
Is this Ascension's sign?

The sun settling quickly beyond the green Georgia pines,
Rays broken in the boughs; rays dancing, bidding farewell
On the still again lake by the Monastery.

Settling, settling, all is descending, not ascending
Here by the lake on Ascension's Eve.
But I know that His ascension comes.

On the morrow His ascension comes,
For my lectionary tells me so,
Here by the lake on the eve of Ascension.

UPSTAIRS

Acts 2

The days since Jesus' execution have passed quickly. Days of fear and confusion and deep sorrow. Days of shock and disappointment that Jesus was not the Messiah most of us thought he was. The crucifixion was indecently perfunctory and brutal. I had seen Jesus once since that dark day on Golgotha. He appeared suddenly to a small group of us gathered for prayer and consolation at a friend's house near Gethsemane. I was not there when he appeared to another group which included the twelve. One of the twelve, my close friend Thomas, told me of touching Jesus wounds to be sure that he was alive again as some had claimed. Yes, I had seen and heard him since I witnessed what was surely his death on the cross, but I still have my doubts. Perhaps I was imagining that I saw him; perhaps in my disillusion, I saw an illusion.

My heart truly aches for him. I loved him so much. I remember being overcome with love in that meeting with him in the garden after he had healed the peasant with the withered arm that Sabbath day. Right then I walked away from my prestigious life as a Pharisee leader when he said simply, "Follow me." In the days that followed any doubts that he was the promised Messiah fell away. I knew he was the Messiah! Now the doubts have returned. To really believe in the resurrection from the dead is difficult. Nothing in my religious training prepared me for this challenge. The twelve often told of another healing. The father of a boy possessed by demons asked Jesus if he could help him. Jesus replied to the father, "If I can?, all things

123

are possible to him who believes." And now I cry out what the father cried out: "I do believe, help my unbelief!"

Although I was open and honest about my doubt about the resurrection, the Apostles, now eleven, called me out along with Matthias as a candidate to replace Judas Iscariot. Perhaps my doubts were the reason the lot had fallen to Matthias and not to me. I was not alone in my doubts, others were still confessing their doubts even after many more reports of a risen Jesus among us.

We had gathered again to pray and wait as he had instructed. 'Wait for what?', I thought. 'To see him again? No, for some of the disciples had seen him ascend up into the clouds last week and there have been no reports of him since. Would he descend from the clouds? The possibility that all of us here have lost our minds resurfaces, proving at least that not all of my mind is gone.

To my surprise, Peter has become a leader among the twelve. He is likable enough but a rather crude country fellow. My patrician prejudice toward the Galileans is surfacing. Peter is again urging everyone to remain and pray and wait as Jesus said. He is a stubborn sort and I wonder if he hides his own doubts beneath this steadfast stance. Joanna, apparently sensing my despair, comes to me. "Joseph, (no one calls me Justus anymore), take heart", she says softly. "Jesus has risen, he has risen indeed!" Joanna was with the women who assisted my friend Joseph of Arimathea in laying Jesus in his tomb and one of the group that went to the tomb on Sunday morning. She remains absolutely certain that he was both dead on Friday and alive again on Sunday. Joanna has a gentle and reassuring spirit that is motherly despite her youth. She was one of a group of women who had followed Jesus since the beginning of his travels. She knew him well and was a convincing witness to his teaching - and now to his death and resurrection. "Jesus promised us that he would give us the power to overcome our fears and doubts. Please, Joseph, take heart,

Jesus loved you very much", she is saying with convincing warmth. "I know, I know", I answer, still unconvinced.

A loud noise like the wind of a fierce storm startles the gathering. I look out the small window above, the sky is clear. What is that noise that is literally shaking the room? Now flickers of light, like fireflies, fill the room. What appears to be sparks of fire are falling from the ceiling. What is going on? I am mad. There is great confusion and shouting but no one is trying to leave. A man from Pontus with whom I had become acquainted rushes up to me exclaiming, "the spirit of God has come upon us!" But wait, how did I know what he said? He spoke only the Pontus language and we had talked through an interpreter before. But now he spoke in my Aramean tongue. Another that I knew to be an Elamite comes to us praising God in Greek, my other language.

I am confused and bewildered. How can this be? I stand in awestruck silence for what seems to be a long time. I seem to be suspended in a trance as the excitement and commotion of the room goes on around me, but somehow apart from me. My confusion melts away and I am overcome with a sense of peace that passes my understanding. A feeling of blessed warmth engulfs me and a glow comes up from within me like that of the now invisible tongues of fire that had filled the room. I recall Jesus saying he was the vine and we are the branches, of his strange teaching about dwelling in us and we in him. I know, in some new way of knowing, that the glow and warmth and peace in me is really Jesus. He is risen indeed! Suddenly, no longer in my suspended state, I too am embracing the others with shouts of "Praise the Lord, Praise the Lord!"

Finally the excitement subsides somewhat and someone asks "What does this mean?" Others pick up the question, "Yes, what does this mean?"

"It means you're drunk" shouts one of a group who have come in from outside to see what the commotion is about. "Yes", mocks another, "they are full of sweet wine!"

The twelve have gathered together in the front of the room and are talking among themselves. Peter rises to speak and immediately gets the attention he requests. Peter, once the crude country boy, has a new countenance. He appears older somehow, no, just more mature. Before he speaks I know I am about to hear the truth about what all this means.

Finis

BOATING WITH JESUS

Acts 8:4-8
Mark 4:35-41

"Philip, you are a gifted evangelist. It seems that all of Samaria is rejoicing in the baptisms you have done. The good news of the spread of the gospel of our Lord Jesus has come to us in Jerusalem." These words from Peter are welcome and encouraging. The other apostles had asked Peter and John to come down from Jerusalem to assist and encourage me as I took the good news of the kingdom of God and the name of Jesus Christ to the people of Samaria.

"Philip, we want you to come back with us to Jerusalem now", says my friend from boyhood, John. "Since they killed Stephen, Saul of Tarsus has led an attack on us. Many are in prison; work is hard to find. It is dangerous but we need your help in Jerusalem."

I protest, "But my work is here in Samaria. We are just getting started with discipling folks about the work of our Lord Jesus."

"You already have many disciples here who will continue spreading the gospel of our Lord Jesus. You have done well. We need you to come", replies John. Peter adds his agreement without speaking; with a piercing, authoritative stare.

I agree to go back to the twelve in Jerusalem. It is clear that Peter and John, and the rest of the twelve, have assumed authority over the so called Jesus movement. I feel a desire to obey them, even though there are many reasons to stay. Peter and John have changed, matured. Peter has surprisingly become a real leader, not only by his courage, but by his passionate and articulate preaching about Jesus. Even John, who I grew up with in our little fishing village by the

Galilee sea, was a different man - wise and compassionate. John, the wild one, who with his brother James, was always leading us into boyhood adventures that usually ended up badly - at least from our parents' point of view. And the final grand adventure of some teenagers tagging along after another new Messiah seemed to end badly too. That is, until the resurrection and the coming of Holy Spirit that day in the upper room.

As the three of us trek toward Jerusalem, now silent in our own thoughts, I think back to that strange day on the sea when John enticed me to come along with Jesus and his followers. What began as another teenage adventure that day by the sea has led me to preaching the coming of the kingdom of God in Jesus Christ just a few years later. I remember the excitement of the crowd as we boarded our boats to follow Jesus, in the lead boat, over toward the Gerasene coast. Jesus had been teaching from a boat facing a large crowd from the surrounding villages. This was the first time I had heard Jesus and I thought his message was very confusing. I had wondered how his odd teaching drew such a crowd. John and James, who had been with Jesus for a while, said that he taught in parables that caused you to think about the meaning of them long after the telling. Then came that amazing voyage across the sea. The images of that evening flooded back into my memory, as real as the water that flooded the boat in the storm...

I was standing with my five boat mates in the knee deep water that flooded the boat during the brief but fierce storm. We stood in awe struck silence before the perfectly still and serene Galilean Sea that had been a raging tempest only moments before. Six teenage boys, experiencing perhaps for the first time the true beauty of the sea that had been by them since their births. The sun was setting behind the western shore of our home and as we looked toward the east the now darkening clear sky began to birth the evening stars.

The sea before us was as a silken tablecloth set for a royal feast. It was the perfect calm.

A breeze from the west rippled the sail and ended our silent meditations. As we began to bail out the nearly sinking boat, my thoughts shifted from beauty to power. I had taken up my fishing duties on the family boat when I was six or seven and was already a veteran seaman at nineteen, like John, James and most of the other boys of the village. I had been caught in some storms, but none like this one. The usual warning signs were absent when we departed. There was a good westerly wind that would get us to the Gerasene coast before nightfall. Suddenly the sky darkened and a fierce wind whipped up huge swells that blotted out sight of the boats around us. Our attempt to lower the sail was useless as we were tossed about in the gale. Miraculously no one went overboard, for surely they would have drowned. As we clung to the floor and sides the warm sea water flooded our small vessel and I thought we surely would sink before the boat broke up. Then, more suddenly than it arose, the storm ceased. The perfect calm.

With a good wind our little flotilla landed shortly. After finding that all had come through the storm safely, John and I retreated to a spot away from the others and talked.

"Philip, you are not going to believe this", John said, excited. "Jesus had gone to the stern and fallen asleep as soon as we cast off. When the storm hit, everyone was holding on for dear life, and I looked back for Jesus and he was still asleep! Someone shook him awake and yelled 'Don't you care that we are dying?'

Jesus stood up, looked out, and as if talking to the wind, said "Hush, be still."

John is both excited and perplexed by the events he is describing. He speaks carefully, as if making sure that he is remembering correctly.

"Then it became very still and calm. Jesus looked around at us and asked us why we were so afraid and had no faith?" John's eyes were now peering into the night sky, as if he were talking to himself, not me. He was now solemn, not excited. John is silent in his thoughts for a long moment.

"Philip", John speaks without breaking off his now distant gaze, "who is he that even the wind and the sea obey him? Why am I afraid even now, after the storm?"

Suddenly, John turned to me with that familiar look of fearless determination. "Philip, weren't you afraid? Who wouldn't be?" He was angry now and still not really talking to me, but arguing with the absent Jesus. "No faith? Faith in what? Was I supposed to know this carpenter could command the wind?" This kind of talk from John often to led to one of our reckless adventures. I wondered where this might take John - and me - for I knew I would follow him again.

"John", I interrupted his one sided debate, "what about the healings and miracles you told me about? Are you doubting his power?"

"No, it's not that. He made this personal, though. He was scolding us. Why would he have expected us not to be afraid? Why did he question our faith? Anyway, what's faith got to do with it?" John's inquisitiveness was overtaking his anger now. But I sense an adventure is still on.

"John, I don't know who he is that has power over the wind and sea, and somehow I am afraid too, and I don't know what faith has to do with it; but I think we should follow him and see if we can find out."

"Oh yes, Philip, we will follow him. This may be the adventure of a lifetime!"

"And what an adventure it is" I hear myself say out loud to no one in particular.

"What's that?", asks Peter, thinking I was talking to him.

"Oh, nothing" I say non-chalantly.

John casts me a knowing smile.

Finis

Discussion Guide
The Rich Young Ruler

I believe "The Rich Young Ruler" is ideally suited for Book Clubs and Bible Study groups. Following are some suggestions for group discussions, or a guide for thinking through the stories on your own. I would love to share in your discussions. You can contact me through Facebook; my Blog http://george-grove.blogspot.com/ and e-mail: geogrove3@embarqmail.com.

1. What is your opinion of the Biblical novel genre, such as "The Rich Young Ruler "? Is this your first reading of such a novel or short story? What are some other writings in this genre?

2. What are the themes in RYR? Forgiveness? Redemption? Quest? Social status? How is "Power" a major theme?
A major theme is adapting to the radical societal change caused by Jesus and his disciples. Who are the "powers" that are aligned and opposed in this struggle? Discuss this in context of Thaddaeus' talk with Ethan about Jesus coming to divide even families; about Jesus and the sword? (pp 65-68). Do you agree with Thaddaeus' rationalization of this? How does this play out in Ethan's family. (Part Five's dialog between Ethan and his mother Livia.)

3. Discuss the bar Ezer family characters in RYR. How would you profile Ethan? Phinehas? Livia? Caleb? Daniel?

4. Ethan, of course, is the protagonist and central character. Discuss his personality and gifts. How does he change as significant events impact him? Is Ethan really a changed person or does God adapt his gifts for a new purpose, a new calling? In Part Three examine Ethan in the context of his meeting with Matthew, Joseph of Arimathea, and Nicodemus of Hebron shortly after Pentecost.

5. Did the Caleb/Stephen transformation surprise you? Was the portrayal of Caleb after his prodigal days consistent with him becoming a saint of loving and caring?

6. How do you assess Phinehas bar Ezer (Abba)? What were his chief traits? Did he adequately represent the 'old guard'?

7. Livia is a key character even though her presence is limited. How do you see her traits? Was she a stronger advocate of the 'old guard' than her husband Phinehas? Livia was certainly a no nonsense, get on with it personality. Was she also loving? If so, where does she show her love?

8. Thaddaeus, the apostle, played a central and important role. But we know basically nothing about him from the Bible. Look up the gospel passages where Jesus calls the twelve. Do you find a consistent identification of Thaddaeus? Was he the son or brother of James? Which James? What other names are given to Thaddaeus?

9. What is your character picture of Thaddaeus? Describe what he looks and sounds like to you? Do his Galilean peasant ways hinder his evangelical spirit with his social superiors? Find and discuss passages where he displays great faith and wisdom. Did you

find Thaddaeus' novel way of story telling enjoyable (pp 55-58 and the Short Stories after RYR)?

10. The episodes in RYR are interwoven around Biblical passages. For example, in Part Four, Amal bar Hiram, the messenger from Jerusalem to Ethan tells of the events generally recorded in Acts 3-5. Read Acts 3-5 and re-read this section of RYR. Is the RYR consistent with the scriptural narrative? Are there significant differences? Another example is Ethan recalling his ancestor Joseph and his sons Manasseh and Ephraim. Find the Biblical account in Genesis and discuss in relation to the RYR.

11. Some of the Hebrew names, but not all, call up Bible passages relative to RYR. Find the names in a good concordance and discus the similarities and differences.

12. George's Big Question! The imaginative experience of putting myself into Bible narratives makes scripture come alive for me. I believe it is a means of grace that deepens my spiritual walk with Jesus Christ. This extension of *Lectio Divina* approaches scripture for formation rather than information. Do you believe this might affect you in a similar way? Will different personality types respond differently? Would you like to know more about *Lectio Divina* after reading The Rich Young Ruler?

CPSIA information can be obtained at www.ICGtesting.com
Printed in the USA
LVOW121117180112

264441LV00001B/5/P